Before Ai

Eric Barger

Contact the author

http://www.EricBarger.me

Twitter @ericbarger

Instagram @AuthorEricBarger

Word Count: 23,428

Copyright © 2019 Eric Barger

Developmental Editor: Savannah Gilbo

Proofreading by WordRefiner.com

Cover Art by Eric Barger © 2019

Back Cover Summary by Aiden Barger © 2019

Ai Rising Illustration by Steven McQuilkin © 2018

ISBN-13: 978-0-578-62831-8 (paperback)

First Edition

0, 1, 1, 2, 3, 5, 8, 13, 21, 34, 55, 89, 144, …

Kelly

To my wife for whom without, this book would not exist.

"Anything is possible." - Aiden Anders

1

PI Day

Taylor studied the circuit board she held, trying to keep her mind off the time. It was past her typical bedtime, but with the adrenaline rushing through her body, sleep was nowhere in sight. Looking at her watch, she stood from her chair in the sitting room and walked past the kitchen towards the study. "It's 10:28 pm. MIT acceptance emails should arrive at any moment."

Her dad put down his Sudoku puzzle as she walked by. "Well, the message has to travel all the way to Durdle Door, England," he said, and Taylor's mom laughed.

Taylor refreshed her email a few times and huffed. "Where is that email?" She opened a new tab in her browser and clicked on a shortcut. Tapping her feet against the floor, she logged on to Professor Davis' message forum to see if anyone had posted any updates.

She scanned the "MIT Acceptance" thread and noticed many members had posted their success stories, but a few had posted they hadn't been accepted into MIT. "Where is my email?" Taylor asked, mumbling more to herself than anyone else. "I won't get accepted. I knew my application wasn't good enough."

A chime sounded, interrupting Taylor's gloomy thoughts. "About time." She paused and took a breath, then wiped her sweaty palms on her pants. Her finger drifted across the track pad and selected the message.

Her mom stepped up behind her and placed a hand on her shoulder, giving an encouraging squeeze. "It will be fine, no matter the outcome. You already have three full scholarships to top British Universities."

"But this is the one I care about." Taylor took a moment to look back at her parents. Taking a deep breath, she opened the email.

Taylor read the opening line of the message aloud. "On behalf of the Admissions Committee, it is my pleasure to offer you admission to the MIT Class of — I'm in. I'm in!"

As her eyes continued scanning the screen, her voice grew louder and giddy. "I also received a scholarship to cover half of my tuition. This is great news!" She jumped up and embraced her parents. "I can't believe I'm in!" Taylor and her parents just stood staring at each other.

They took a moment to celebrate and chat about this exciting news.

They took a seat near the computer, and her dad peered over his glasses. "Do you have a friend or classmate from school you want to message with the good news?"

"I do! Hamburglar."

"Who?" asked her dad with furrowed brows.

"Hamburglar. It's a nickname used by a member on the forum." She felt silly about it and her insides were full of butterflies, but she had regarded Hamburglar as a good friend since they had connected on Professor Davis' message forum. Taylor's greatest wish was to attend MIT and finally have a friend to whom she could relate. "Give me one second to let Hamburglar know." She sat down and her fingers hit the keyboard with a series of fast clicks. "There. All done. I'll catch up on the forum tomorrow."

Before she had a chance to stand, a new message popped up in Taylor's inbox. "I have another message in the system. It's from the admissions department." She leaned back in her chair. "Why would they send me another message? Do you think there has been a mistake? Did they realize I received an acceptance letter in error?" Her mind frantically started considering all the possible reasons for another email so soon after her acceptance email.

"Open it," her mom said. "Staring at it won't tell

you anything."

Taylor opened and skimmed the message. "Due to my age, I'm required to attend a second interview. It has to be a face-to-face meeting during Campus Preview Weekend. They want to be sure I can live on my own and handle college. Being young complicates everything."

"An in-person meeting?" her mom asked as she rubbed her eyes.

"They're right to do that. Fourteen is too young to go so far away from home. Your mom and I really want you closer to home."

Taylor's mouth started to open. Pausing for a moment, she continued reading the message on the screen. "Oh my. My meeting is with Professor Davis. That can't be right. She is much too important to meet with incoming freshmen."

"Why would you say that?" her dad asked.

"I mean, I'm just surprised that Professor Davis would be the one to conduct the in-person interview to determine if I'm ready for the transition to college. She's not just any person. She is THE person when it comes to artificial intelligence. She's bigger than a big deal, and I'm just a kid."

"Stop putting yourself down," her mom said. "Professor Davis may be a superhero in your eyes, but she's still just a person like the rest of us."

"Thanks, mom. It's just a little overwhelming to think about my hero deciding my dream." Her voice faded. "Besides — "

"Besides," her mom picked up where Taylor had trailed off, "MIT is expensive, and we can't take on that kind of debt."

Taylor's head dropped when she heard the reality of the situation. It was the absolute worst time to discuss money. She just received the best news of her life, and her mom's simple statement poured cold water over her exciting news. She took her hands off the keyboard and turned to face her parents.

Her mom stole a look at her dad. "Taylor, why are you still chasing MIT when you have full scholarships to top universities here, closer to home? Your dad and I want you to chase your dreams, but we also have to be financially sensible."

"Even with half of your tuition being paid, we can't afford the remaining tuition," her dad said. "And this trip to MIT would be a few thousand dollars in flights, lodging, and food. And that's if only one of us accompanies you. That trip will prevent us from visiting my family in Hong Kong, and I haven't seen my parents, your grandparents, in years," her dad said with a tired look in his eyes.

Her mom cleared her throat. "We also can't forget

the cost of a new roof, which needs to be replaced before fall."

Taylor felt like her heart was shrinking. "If I attend school here at home, I wouldn't be in the company of like minds. I can relate to the people on the message forum. Working with Hamburglar has shown me just how good life can be if I'm surrounded by the right people. And Professor Davis is the best in the world, and I'd be stupid to pass up this opportunity."

Her dad opened his mouth to speak when Taylor cut him off. "I've spent the last nine months taking part in monthly coding challenges on Professor Davis' forum. There have been nine challenges, and twice I have finished in the top three." She sat up as tall as she could. "I have one more online challenge to complete before I can qualify for a seat at the coding competition during Campus Preview Weekend. Professor Davis awards a scholarship to the top three students in the coding competition."

Keeping an impassive face, Taylor's mom asked the obvious question. "If you win this competition, will you get all the money you need to go to MIT?"

Taylor took a deep breath. She wasn't sure she could win them over. She couldn't blame them for wanting to see Grandma and Grandpa or for needing to fix the roof. She ran her fingers through her hair, rougher than she had intended and grimaced. "It's a last dollar scholarship with a stipend. It will cover any remaining tuition plus some extra. I've worked so hard to get to this point, and I don't want to let my dream go until I've done everything I can."

Her dad leaned back in his chair, turning to look at Taylor's mom. An unspoken conversation seemed to pass between them. She was sure they communicated telepathically, but she could never figure out how. "Taylor, your mom and I believe in you. We do want you to chase your dreams." He looked at her mom, and she gave an almost imperceptible nod. Inhaling deeply, he continued. "If you qualify for Professor Davis' competition, we will borrow the money and take you to Campus Preview Weekend…"

"Thank you! Thank you! I'm so grateful for — "

Her dad raised his hand to quiet her, and Taylor's breath hitched. "If you don't receive the remaining scholarship money by the end of that week, you must attend one of the universities closer to home." He stood from his chair and extended his hand.

Taylor didn't take her parents' ultimatum lightly. She stared at his extended hand and looked at her mom. "You mean it?" Taylor asked.

"We mean it," her mom responded with a warm smile and a twinkle in her eyes. "We're willing to bet the roof on it."

They were offering her a one-shot deal, which was a huge risk. Her performance hadn't been as good as she had hoped in the challenges. She raised her right hand and it stilled a few inches from her father's. For a moment she considered walking away from her dream because of the hardship she would place on her family. "You have a deal." She grabbed her dad's hand before she could change her mind.

"Thank you! I won't let you down, and I'll make this up to you. I promise." Taylor stood up and hugged her parents. She started to leave the room but stopped in the doorway and looked back at her parents. "Maybe I can meet Hamburglar if I go to MIT in April."

A tight-lipped smile showed on her mom's face. "As long as one of us is there to meet this Hamburglar, too."

Taylor made her way up to her bedroom and sat down on the bed. She grabbed her tablet and searched the forum for past coding challenge winners. They always posted the challenge's problem plus the winning solution for members to view. She had to gain any insight or edge over the competition she could. Tomorrow was the last qualifying challenge, the one that would determine her fate.

2

Einstein's Birthday

Aiden stood by the dining table watching the time tick by on the kitchen clock. 6:26 pm. Two more minutes until he found out if he'd be going to MIT this fall. "Albert Einstein's birthday. I think that's a funny time to release acceptance letters."

Aiden's mom slid the tray of potatoes into the oven. "I found it amusing too. Your dad said he would expect nothing less from a school like MIT."

Aiden smiled. "PI day at Tau time. I don't think it gets any more M-I-T than that." He looked at his mom. "Did you know that Stephen Hawking passed away on PI Day?"

"I didn't, though it adds to the mystique."

"It's almost like the universe was trying to tell us something." Aiden stretched his arms and tried to relax. "What do you think MIT will say?"

"I think things will work out for the best either way," she said. "I wish you had spent the last two hours outside with the neighbor kids instead of watching the clock. As they say, a watched pot never boils."

"Mom, this is all I can think about."

"Aiden, the neighbor boy down the street is one of the few kids you interact with. You won't see him very often once you are off to college. Make the most of it. Friendships are so important for a boy your age." She set the pot holders down on the counter top. "Most thirteen-year-old boys would be outside playing. Don't let this season of your life pass you by."

"Ok. Ok, but tomorrow." Aiden raised both hands. "I need to get logged in, so I know the instant the news arrives." Aiden headed toward the study and sat down at his desk. His insides had that feeling you get when the roller coaster descends faster than you want. It all comes down to this moment. He wiped his brow.

Aiden clicked the mouse, but the screen remained blank. He pecked on the keyboard, but still nothing happened. "Is there something wrong with this computer?"

His dad walked over to the computer and stood beside Aiden. "Did you try the power button?"

Embarrassed, Aiden reached around the large screen and pushed the power button. "I guess that should have been the next thing to check after clicking the mouse and tapping the keyboard."

His dad laughed and rubbed the top of Aiden's head. "I have several lifetimes of experience on you. I also saw the clock blinking on the oven."

Aiden heard his mom's footsteps approaching from the kitchen, and she walked into the study a moment later. He worked the mouse and keyboard with speed. He could feel his pulse beating inside his head. The closer he came to finding out if MIT had accepted him, the less he could think clearly.

He felt his parents hovering behind him. It seems I am not the only one who is interested in my future. He smiled as he opened the browser and logged into his MIT account. "I have a message!"

His mom placed her hand on his shoulder. Aiden could feel the warmth from it, which calmed him. "No matter what the outcome, you have been accepted to plenty of good schools, and this one acceptance is not indicative of your success or failure."

"I know. I know." The screen updated and displayed the message. His eyes moved back and forth across the screen. "I'm in!" He pumped his fist in the air. "This will be the best year ever!" His fist fell and hovered over the keyboard. "I need to let Vesuvius know I'm in." He brought up Professor Davis' message forum in the browser. "They've already started an acceptance thread! Wow, a lot of people got in!" He squinted as he scrolled through the thread. "Hmm. I don't see anything from Vesuvius yet. I hope he made it because I am hoping to meet him during Campus Preview Weekend."

"This is the person you have been working with on some of your projects?" his dad asked.

His dad raised an eyebrow, "Is he as good as you?"

"He's a fast coder who catches mistakes, but he lacks the confidence he needs to really push forward." Aiden stood up and took a few deep breaths, letting it sink in. I can't believe I got in, he thought as he jumped into the air, losing one of his green Crocs as he kicked up his feet. He gave each of his parents a hug. He felt like he had just won ten Olympic gold medals.

His mom faced Aiden holding him at arm's length. "We are very proud of you, buddy."

"You received another message after your acceptance letter," his dad said. "You may want to camp out in front of your messages for more than a few seconds at a time."

"They are probably sending me travel instructions." Aiden sat down and looked at the screen. The email subject line reads, "Dual Major Request." His smile faded into a straight line.

He opened the message and quickly scanned its

contents. "I have a required in-person meeting with Professor Davis because of my age." Aiden's voice trailed off. "I didn't get approved for a dual major like I wanted." His hand hit a puzzle cube, knocking it off the desk.

"Don't worry about the dual major request," his mom said. "CMU has already offered you everything you've asked for. Why not go there instead?"

"Because CMU isn't filled with the people I believe are like me. CMU doesn't have that sense of community and belonging."

"I believe you would find it is filled with people exactly like you."

"Your mom's right," his dad said. "CMU is filled with similar-minded students and teachers. We already knew MIT doesn't allow students to declare a major, much less a second one, until the spring semester of their freshman year. The chances of receiving approval for a second degree were highly unlikely. Don't make this difficult. You should give both CMU and Stanford serious consideration."

"CMU is a good school, but it's not where I want to go. I told you that already," Aiden's face was turning red.

"Can you at least give it some more thought? You have a full ride and then some to the other schools already. There's no rush to decide," his dad said.

His mom sat down and opened the book that had been laying on the table. "We are proud of you for being accepted to the school you wanted. Don't let this dual major request become the hill you die on."

Aiden was sensitive about receiving too much unrealistic positivity. Because of this, his mom was encouraging but remained realistic. He appreciated her not being over the top, like most parents of kids his age.

"MIT is the center of the AI world and nothing less will do. It is THE school to attend if you are serious about AI. They also have Professor Davis. That's where I want to study."

"Don't be so serious about school and forget there is more to the experience than grades." She held up a book. "I got a little nostalgic today and thought back to my time in college. This is one of my yearbooks from college."

Aiden stood beside his mom as she flipped through the book. "Is that you? Who is that with you?"

Laughing, his mom pointed to herself on the page. "That's Olivia Baker and me. We were best friends in college."

"I don't remember ever hearing about her. Do you still talk to her?"

Aiden's dad cleared his throat and motioned for the yearbook. "Let's see if we can find me in this book.

Wait until you see what kind of hair I had back then."

His mom rubbed her palms on her jeans and stood up. "I'm headed back to the kitchen to finish up dinner. You two come join me in a few minutes." His mom stopped and turned to Aiden. "You can't worry about this and let it drag you down. Just be the best Aiden you can be." Aiden nodded as he watched his mom walk out of the room.

Aiden turned and looked at his dad. "When I talked to MIT several months back, I made it clear how I felt about a dual major. With NASA's announced timeline regarding the Mars Mission Colony, I need two degrees to make my application stand out from those of other applicants to the program. Not counting the three years of professional experience I have to get before applying. Four years at MIT and three years of professional experience gives me only a one-year cushion to meet NASA's deadline. I want to be one of the first humans to colonize Mars. I have to be, dad."

"I believe you can achieve your dream through CMU," his dad said. "And you're already accepted with a dual major at CMU."

"Outside of the armed forces, MIT has produced more astronauts than any other university. That doesn't mean I wouldn't be able to become an astronaut by attending a school like CMU or Stanford. It's just not the path I want to take." He was still trying to figure out why MIT denied his dual major request. It can't be my grades, test scores. "Do you think they denied me a dual major because of my age? I will be fourteen when the first day of school rolls around."

Aiden's dad shrugged.

"I realize a lot of kids want to be scientists and astronauts. Not every kid has a shot at attending MIT. Surely, they can see my point-of-view on this." Aiden said, staring hard at the screen.

"Your academics are good enough, and your coding skills are great. I'm sure they have rules in place. Just get in touch with the school and ask them why they turned you down. That seems like the most straightforward solution." He rubbed his forehead. "Remember, CMU is a top-notch school. Just think about it."

"You always say there are exceptions to every rule, dad. This time, I think I can be that exception."

Sighing, his dad said, "You believe you are the exception to every rule. That's what makes you so impossible sometimes."

Maybe Vesuvius will have an opinion. Plus, I want to see if he's willing to meet up during Campus Preview Weekend.

Aiden's dad tapped him on the shoulder and

motioned for him to get moving. "Until then, we better get in the kitchen. You know how your mom gets when we aren't ready to eat as soon as the food is on the table. Besides, she fixed your favorite. Hamburgers."

"Dinner is on the table you two," his mom called from the kitchen.

"We're on our way. One second. I need to check something." Aiden scrolled down a web page, eyes wide to take in as many words as possible. "Yes! His update just posted to the forum. Vesuvius was accepted into MIT!" Aiden smiled. "I will pursue MIT until they get sick of me."

3

Race Day

Aiden leaned against the 2005 Corvette while looking around the drag strip. "Dad, I'm glad you brought me out here today."

"You looked like you needed to get away from everything. Disconnect."

Aiden covered his ears, protecting them from the noise as two cars raced down the drag strip. "Tell me this never gets old." The sound from the track shook his insides like drum beats, one after another.

His dad reached over and rubbed the top of Aiden's head and chuckled. "It never gets old. Unless you break something. Then it gets old."

Aiden pulled his phone out of his pocket, tapped it a few times and focused on the screen. "Dang it. That's not what I wanted to hear."

"Everything ok?" Aiden's dad asked.

"First world problems, dad. I sent a message to Professor Davis last night. Aiden put his phone back in his pocket and ran his fingers through his hair. "She says I can present a project of my choosing, but it has to tie computer science and radio astronomy together. A panel of three professors will review the project during Campus Preview Weekend. Even if I can impress them, my chances are still slim for a dual major. I'd need something ready by early April."

"That's not a lot of time." His dad adjusted the large torque wrench he was holding. "Any idea what kind of project you would present if you decide to go through with it?"

"I don't have anything in mind, which is another problem."

His dad wiped his hands on a rag and placed it in his back pocket. "You could just attend CMU. Problem solved." He smacked his hands together. "Hey, that looks like Oliver and his dad a few spots over. Why don't you go say hi?"

Aiden nodded and made his way over to Oliver and his dad. They were working on a 1967 Chevy II, getting it ready to race. "Hey, Mr. Scott. Hi, Oliver."

"Hey," Oliver said. "You bring the Vette?"

"Yeah."

"Will you make it down the track today with your

custom tune?"

"It's more than custom tune. CIRE is artificial intelligence."

"Sounds like a tune to me. I don't get the big deal you make it out to be. Even I can go in and push a bunch of buttons and call it a tune. It takes someone who really knows what they're doing to make it work."

"Cars today receive information from a bunch of sensors while running. The car's computer cross-references the data from the sensors against a pre-populated lookup table, which presents a predetermined value to maximize combustion cycles based on octane tolerance." Aiden started to pace back and forth. "CIRE analyzes each combustion cycle of the motor with real-time thought. Absolute power at wide-open-throttle."

Oliver turned his head and spit to the side. "The last few times you tried your tune something has went wrong every time. You ain't even made any passes down the track yet. You should just hire a guy like we did. They can tune it over the internet these days."

Aiden let out a long sigh. "It's more than a tune, Oliver."

"So, are you going to try out your custom tune today or not? You never answered the question. I can't imagine your dad wanting to get towed off the starting line again."

"Uh, I don't think so." Aiden's eyes dropped toward the ground and then glanced back up at Oliver. "You want to check out the other cars with me?" Aiden pointed to a car a few spaces over. "There's a '68 Nova over there with flames painted all over it. It's pretty cool."

Oliver pointed at Aiden's feet. "I'm not walking around with you while you're wearing those stupid shoes. People will laugh at us."

"Be nice," Oliver's dad snickered.

Aiden shrugged and took a few steps back. "Never mind. Just thought I would ask." He turned and walked back to his car. As he approached his dad, Aiden said, "Oliver's busy."

"Attention test-n-tune cars. Make your way to the staging lanes," the announcer called out.

His dad walked around to the rear of the car and opened the hatch. "That's us. I think you need to fire up CIRE. I have a feeling that today will be different. Besides, you need to test your latest updates."

Aiden didn't waste any time walking around the car to meet his dad. "Really? Are you serious?"

"I'm serious. Do what you need to do, and let's see what happens."

A crooked smile appeared on Aiden's face. "I'll get the computers booted and cables connected. Won't take two minutes."

Aiden powered on the notebook computers, which acted as the brain for the car's operation. He made his way to the front passenger seat and opened the glove box to connect the specialty interface cables to bypass the car's PCM. He plugged in the final cable and did a quick diagnostic test on the computer. Looking good! "Start it up, dad!"

Aiden explained, "The car will run off CIRE to maximize performance, but the PCM will still handle the gauge cluster so we can see our speed and rpm."

As he turned the key, his dad said, "That's a nice improvement." The car started without hesitation. "I think you're onto something this time, Aiden."

"Couldn't have done it without a little help from Vesuvius in that last update."

"Maybe we will make it down the track this time." His dad reached into the center console. "Let's get our tech card turned in and find a lane so we can test it out."

After receiving their number, they were directed to lane three. A Mustang pulled up beside them in lane four to their left. Heat waves created a mirage off the hot, concrete starting line. Aiden's chest tightened.

The race starter turned and pointed to each car, giving them each a thumbs up. The Mustang pulled into the burnout box first, and Aiden listened to its engine thunder.

With no notice, the Corvette roared to life. White smoke billowed from underneath the tires. The car started to roll forward. Letting off the accelerator, the tires screeched against the concrete as they left the water box.

Aiden looked down at his computer screen. "Hmm."

As soon as the Mustang rolled into the first light, Aiden's dad set off the second and final staging light. He brought the Corvette up to 4,000 rpm on the foot-brake, ready to launch. "Everything feels good. How does it look on the computer?"

Aiden looked at his dad, raised his helmet's visor and yelled, "Uhh." He banged his hand against the side of the computer hoping the numbers would change for the better. "CIRE's logic appears confused."

"Should I be worried?" his dad shouted over the engine noise.

"Probably!"

As the Mustang staged, both cars strained to prevent their imminent, violent launch off the line. The three rows of amber lights on the Christmas tree came on all at once. Aiden saw the green light when his head hit the back of the seat as the Corvette shot forward.

"Whoa! CIRE is working!" Aiden's dad yelled as he pulled back on the shifter to put the car in second gear. A chirp came from the drag radials spinning on the sticky track surface.

Aiden glanced over to his left looking for the Mustang. His helmet obstructed his peripheral vision, but he could tell the Mustang was far behind them. "It's working! I can't believe it. I thought the processing power would be too slow once we started down the track."

The car accelerated through the finish line, and the clock flashed their time.

"Six tenths of a second! We picked up six tenths." His dad pumped his fist and let off the accelerator, allowing the car to slow itself down before reaching the end of the track. He leaned forward, looking in his side mirror. "We put a hundred feet on him! Whoo! Good job, son!"

Aiden loosened the grip on the computer and puffed his chest out a little. "I knew it would work today! I need to thank Vesuvius for helping me with that update!" He slid his hand over toward his dad for a low five congratulations.

Once they reached the pit area, Aiden pulled his helmet off and threw it behind the seats. He looked up and noticed an odd-looking ham radio antenna on the top of a trailer parked near them.

"Dad, I think inspiration may have struck." Aiden snapped his fingers.

"Yeah. How so?" His dad tossed his helmet in the

cargo area behind the seats, got out of the car and walked around to the passenger side, stretching his back as he walked.

"A thought just popped into my head about using CIRE in real time to search for alien life. A project connecting computer science and radio astronomy for my MIT presentation. It might be possible…"

"You only just got CIRE to work for the first time today. It sounds risky. Maybe go with something more simple that's sure to perform?"

"It would be a gamble, for sure."

"A gamble you don't need to take."

"If it works, and that is a big if, the payoff would be enormous." Aiden got lost in his thoughts, staring ahead at nothing in particular. "I'm going to adapt CIRE to find alien radio signals."

4

Late Start

Taylor rolled over and tapped her phone's screen. The screen came into focus as she rubbed her eyes. "I'm late!" She jumped out of bed and pulled her hair into a quick ponytail as she ran down the stairs and through the kitchen.

Her mom yelled, "What's the hurry?"

"The challenge started at seven." She landed in her chair with her feet circling the floor looking for her favorite insulated slippers. "Ugh, it's freezing in here!" Taylor looked outside and saw snow on the ground.

"Taylor, you need to eat breakfast first," her mom said. "You need to put your slippers on. You know how cold feet distract you."

Taylor stuffed her earbuds into her ears and opened the forum for the coding challenge instructions. Her eyes glanced at the upper right hand corner of her screen. "Fifteen 'til nine."

She could choose one of two challenges to work. "Efficiently packing a container full of different-sized parts or text recognition." Without a doubt, packing a container would be the easiest problem for her to solve in the time remaining.

She jumped when her mom set a plate down beside her. Eggs and bacon, her favorites.

"You need to eat," her mom said. "One can't expect to do well on an empty stomach."

Taylor stared at the runny eggs and bacon on her plate. Her mom wasn't the best cook. She hesitated. "I'll eat in a few minutes."

Her mom turned and left the room as quietly as she had entered.

As Taylor watched her mom head toward the kitchen, a notification sound drew her attention back to the screen. It was a message from Professor Davis' forum. "I am glad you decided to join the rest of us, Vesuvius. Try not to go down in ashes. P.S. Do a search for HSL. - David Hill."

HSL. What could that possibly mean? Taylor brought up her favorite search engine and typed in HSL. She clicked search and froze as the results populated the screen. "This can't be." Hill Shipping & Logistics Ltd, based out of Australia, was the second largest shipping container company in the world. It's obvious his family doesn't need a scholarship for him to attend MIT, much less any school. He probably only enters the challenges to prove to everyone how smart he is. Ugh!

Her fist slammed down, jarring her glass and causing a few drops of water to escape. "Shoot!" She took a slow, deep breath.

"Of all the problems to solve, it would have to be this one. Of all the days to oversleep! No doubt David will do well since his family is in shipping and logistics."

David Hill was without question THE biggest jerk she had ever encountered. She didn't understand why Professor Davis allowed David Hill to remain on the forum. Not only did he not need a scholarship, but he was also a bully. I thought Professor Davis had an anti-bullying policy.

David's constant barrage of belittling comments to Taylor throughout the coding challenges had been a huge motivating factor for her to put in extra time before each challenge. She had made it her goal to beat him on at least one challenge but had only come close on the last two attempts. A sick feeling grew in her stomach as she read the challenge, knowing it would play into David's forte. What was the point? She took a deep breath and realized her fists were clenched. Getting mad won't solve anything. All she needed was a top ten finish to guarantee a seat at the coding competition during Campus Preview Weekend. Her chances of finishing that high in today's challenge were dwindling by the moment.

Taylor considered her options. Stick with your first instinct. Beat David Hill at his own game. You've got this.

The problem would be a challenge to solve. Taylor knew if it was easy, Professor Davis wouldn't call it a challenge. She would need to key in the dimensions for forty-one unique parts and create an algorithm to determine the smallest amount of raw material waste.

I can do this. She pulled out a notepad and drew out the problem on paper. Planning out her approach to the problem would save time. Everything can be solved. It's just another simple problem. Look for patterns. Nothing to worry about. Focus.

When Taylor finally checked the time again, she had one hour remaining. A sound chimed on the computer. Another message. Everyone on the forum knows not to message anyone during a challenge.

"Vesuvius, I'm just putting the final touches on my code. Piece of advice. Be sure you know what language you're coding in before you push submit. But what am I saying? Your progress is probably more like flowing lava on Pompei. - David Hill." Total jerk! I asked one question over a year ago on the forum confusing my programming languages, and he won't drop it!

She shook her head and looked over at the clock. Pausing only when she needed to look up a specific programming syntax, Taylor maintained a steady pace for the next hour.

The timer on the code window popped up, showing the countdown from 60 seconds. "Less than a minute to go." Perspiration beaded on Taylor's forehead as her fingers raced to finish. "End. $CalcWaste.quit. End."

The window closed. She smacked her palm on the desk. "Finished. Ugh, I wish I had more time to iron out a few rough spots. All I can do now is wait."

A message popped up from Hamburglar.

I am sure you did great regardless of your late start. Big D was on the forum before the challenge even ended bragging about how he "smashed" the challenge. He's such a jerk! Let me know how you did. Taylor let the message linger in her mind for a moment.

"Who are you talking to?" her mom asked.

"Mom! You snuck up on me," Taylor said, placing her hand over her heart. "I was reading a message from my friend, Hamburglar, on the forum. He always sends a quick note after the challenge is over asking how it went." She was not sure if the message was an automated script or if he was actually at the keyboard waiting to send. Either way, she was impressed by his consistency.

"You haven't forgotten about our rule have you?

No sharing personal information with strangers." her mom said, rubbing the back of her neck.

"I haven't forgotten, Mom."

"So, you don't know Hamburglar's real name, but you know David Hill's? Why is that?"

Taylor looked at her mom wondering what she was getting at. "Almost everyone uses a pseudonym as their name on the forum. Stranger danger, mom. Only a select few use their real names. David Hill is one of those few. He wants everyone to know his name."

"I see. I think." Her mom's gaze lingered on Hamburglar's open message on the screen. "Is this Hamburglar a boy or girl?"

"I don't know for sure." Taylor pushed a strand of hair away from her eyes. "I have always assumed Hamburglar is a he. I guess Hamburglar could be a she. It's never come up."

"What is your pseudonym?"

"Vesuvius, and that is all anyone knows about me." Looking at her mom through narrowed eyes, she gave herself a moment to think. "Now that you mention it, it sounds weird, but not weird, all at the same time."

"And you and this Hamburglar… you work together on projects?" her mom asked.

"Yeah. And no, I have no idea how old he or she is." She shrugged and rubbed her hands over her face, trying to erase any doubts about her future at MIT.

Taylor's mom cleared her throat. "How long before you know where you placed?"

Taylor sighed and leaned her head back. "Usually, within a few hours. The process is automated. I assume she is running an AI to judge the winners. It's cool actually."

Taylor's dad came in with his arms full of groceries. "How did your coding challenge go? What did I miss?"

"I overslept. It went downhill from there, dad."

"I'm sorry to hear that."

An alert sounded through her speakers. "We are about to find out. I just received a message from Professor Davis." Taylor leaned forward toward the screen. "This can't be right."

"What does it say?" her mom asked.

"I can't believe I beat David Hill." Taylor's hands pressed against her cheeks. "I placed first out of the one hundred and three participants. I've never beat David Hill before!" Taylor shouted with a huge smile. She leaped up from her seat to give her parents high fives.

"The next time Hamburglar tells me anything is possible, I might have to agree with him! I still can't believe it."

"It bothers me you can hear that from a stranger

and believe it, but you can't believe it coming from your own parents," her mom said.

A sly smile spread across her dad's face. "I guess this means we're headed to MIT."

"I need to tell Hamburglar I'll definitely be at Campus Preview Weekend. It would be nice to finally meet in person."

Taylor thought back on today's challenge. "I thought for sure I needed more time to polish a few areas on today's challenge. I guess I got lucky." She tugged on her shirt. "I hope I'm able to perform as well when I get to the coding competition."

5

32-G636

"I have it all planned out." Aiden walked backward on the sidewalk as he talked to his parents. "I'm going to make a great first impression, and that starts with a firm handshake. Then we move to introductions, and after that, I'll finally get to talk about my project." He leapt into the air and landed softly. "Oh man, I can't wait for Professor Davis to hear about my project!" Aiden punched his fist into the palm of his hand. "I can't believe Professor Davis is the one doing my second interview."

"It sounds like you have used the past month wisely," his dad said with a laugh.

His mom put her arm around him. "Have you changed your mind about the mixer?"

"No. I don't want to go. I want to do well on my presentation and meet Vesuvius. That's it." Aiden stopped. Looking up, he smiled. "This building is crazy looking."

"The building has a name, Aiden. It's called the Ray and Maria Stata Center," his mom said. "It looks more like a carnival fun house. I certainly didn't expect anything like this at MIT."

"Do you think the building is this way on the inside too?" his dad asked.

"I can't wait to find out," Aiden said.

"32-G636. Eve A. Davis. This is Professor Davis' office. Identifying buildings by number at MIT is a long-standing practice that I think is weird. No other school we've visited does that," Aiden said after reading the door. "A real shame the inside of the building didn't match the outside." Turning to look at his parents, he motioned with his hand to the open door. "Shall we?"

"Yes, you shall," came a voice from inside the room.

Aiden flinched at the unexpected response and peeked in. "Hello?" Not immediately seeing anyone, Aiden turned to look at the other office doors. He shrugged at his parents. "Hmm. Weird." He took a step inside the doorway and froze.

"Hello, Aiden. I see you found my office," Professor Davis said as she hung her jacket on the hook behind the door.

Professor Davis was shorter in stature, with shoulder length black hair overtaken by gray strands.

"Oh. Hey there, Professor Davis. Yes, we made it just fine," Aiden responded with a nervous laugh. "These are my parents."

Professor Davis motioned to the chairs in front of her desk. Aiden saw her eyes go straight to his green Crocs as he sat down in the middle chair. He tucked his feet behind the chair legs and pretended to look through his backpack for a notebook.

"Nice shoes," Professor Davis said. "Green is a great color. Personally, I prefer orange." She lifted her feet above the desk to show Aiden her orange pair of Crocs.

Professor Davis is the coolest! "Wow, those are cool, too!" He looked at her socks. "Hey, did you know your socks don't match?" Aiden said.

"Yep! And I love them precisely because they don't match. It's more fun that way!" She adjusted her glasses and said, "So, Aiden, let's get started with our meeting."

"I can't believe you take student visits," Aiden said. "I thought you would be way too busy."

"It's a nice way to meet new people." Smiling, she changed the direction of the conversation. "Anyway, about your dual major request, Hamburglar. Have you created a project to wow the panel?"

Aiden cleared his throat. "I believe so. I had a moment of inspiration not long after receiving the news I got into MIT. What did — ”

"Wonderful. I can't wait to see it as I'm sure it will impress. On that note, I'd like to convince you not to press the dual major request."

"What?" Aiden looked from his parents to Professor Davis. "I worked hard to create this project specifically to impress the panel so I could pursue a dual major. Why should I drop it now?"

"Well, you'll be fourteen when you walk through these doors as a freshman. It's a big adjustment for someone your age. Heck, it's an adjustment for most eighteen-year-olds." She looked across the desk at Aiden's parents.

"The projects Aiden completed and posted on the forum were phenomenal, Mr. and Mrs. Anders. You have quite an amazing son."

"But what does that have to do with me dropping my dual major request?"

"Well, I thought concentrating solely on computer science would take your coding skills to a higher level." She leaned back in her chair. "You're a prodigy, Aiden. Maybe even a savant. Your outside the box thinking combined with your coding abilities make you special. I haven't seen an incoming student with your qualifications in many years." She paused for a moment. "Although, come to think of it, we have another bright 14-year-old student who will join our MIT family this fall."

Professor Davis consulted her tablet and looked back at Aiden. "If you drop your request for a second major, I can offer you a research assistant position in MIT's radio astronomy program. You'd have a much easier course load, and the experience would look very impressive on your Mars Colony Mission résumé."

Aiden was only half listening. Did she say there was a second young person entering MIT this fall? "I'm sorry, Professor Davis. Back up a moment. Did you say another young person like me?"

"I did. This student will be in computer science as well, if everything works out. I can introduce you two this weekend, if you'd like." She peered down at her tablet for a moment. "Don't forget, astronaut candidates must also have skills in leadership, teamwork, and communications."

Aiden didn't know what to say. Was this other student on Professor Davis' forum? What if it's David Hill?

"Professor Davis, what's the other student's name?" Aiden asked.

A gasp and the sound of books hitting the hallway floor interrupted their conversation.

"It sounds like someone is having a bad day. One moment." Professor Davis stood up and walked to the open door. "Ah, Professor Baker, is everything ok?"

"Yes. I'm just trying to carry too much. That's all," Professor Baker said.

"Here, let me help you," Professor Davis offered. Aiden looked at his parents. His mom was staring toward the door, bright red and fidgeting with her necklace. "Mom, are you okay?" Aiden asked.

"Yes, I'm fine. It's just a little warm in here is all." She fanned herself with the campus brochure.

Professor Davis shut her office door and said, "Sorry about that. Now, what was I saying? Oh, yes, the research assistant position." She walked around her desk and sat in her chair. "Being a research assistant in the radio astronomy program would give you access to innovative research. I believe it would be a good fit and open up many opportunities down the road."

Aiden slumped back into his seat. Being a research assistant in MIT's radio astronomy program might look just as good as a second degree in physics on my application to NASA. "I do love radio astronomy, and it would be an awesome experience and look great on my application."

"So, is that a yes?" Professor Davis asked with raised eyebrows. "I can cancel your project presentation; although, I would still like to see what you created. You and your parents can enjoy the rest of the weekend, taking in the activities without this big decision hanging over your head. What do you say?"

I can't miss out on being one of the first humans on Mars. NASA misses most of its original timeline estimates, but I have to be ready if they are on schedule. A dual major is more difficult and more likely to impress NASA. But, Professor Davis is right. If I stick with one major and became a research assistant in the radio astronomy program, they could still accept me. Is it worth taking the risk for an easier workload? If I don't get accepted into NASA's Mars program, will I look back on this decision with regret?

Aiden glanced at his parents. His mom had that look moms get when they disapprove of something they know you will do but haven't done yet. How does she always know exactly what I'm thinking? His dad opened his eyes in an exaggerated stare. It was a telepathic plea for him to accept Professor Davis' offer.

"Thank you for the offer, Professor Davis, but my answer is no. I'll see you at the panel for my project presentation," Aiden said, knowing his presentation had to be great.

Professor Davis looked at him for a moment with her hand on her chin. Finally, she stood from her chair and extended her hand. "I look forward to seeing your presentation, Aiden. I wish you the best of luck." A pained expression crossed Professor Davis' face.

He was sure he had let Professor Davis down. "I'll be ready, Professor."

"Don't forget what I said about friends. Especially now that you've decided to pursue a dual major. It will not be easy, but you'll have an easier time if you create a good support system. I look forward to seeing you at my mixer tomorrow night."

"About your mixer," Aiden said. "Uh. I am…" Aiden's words trailed off. He knew what he had to do even if it wasn't what he wanted to do. "I won't forget what you've said. I'll be at the mixer."

6

Electrical Engineering?

Taylor and her parents stood outside Professor Davis' office. She couldn't believe it had already been a month since she first heard the news of her acceptance.

"It's Thursday, correct?" Taylor asked.

"Are you ready?" her dad asked.

"What? Sorry. Yes. I'm ready," Taylor replied. Except, she wasn't ready, and she was nervous about meeting Professor Davis. "What if I don't live up to her expectations? Or worse, what if she says I'm not cut out for MIT?" Both parents looked at her. Taylor shifted her weight from one foot to the other. "It's just a huge deal."

"It's okay to be nervous," her dad said. "But you must have confidence in yourself. If you don't believe in yourself, how can you expect Professor Davis to believe in you?"

She looked up as the door swung open. "Good

morning, Hart family. Please come in." Professor Davis stepped to the side and made a sweeping gesture into the room with her arm.

Taylor couldn't help but notice Professor Davis' hot pink glasses, which stood out like a sore thumb against her otherwise black, business attire. She's so cool! Taylor thought, noticing her orange Crocs and mismatched socks.

"It's great to meet you," Taylor said, pointing to Professor Davis' feet. "I love your socks!"

Professor Davis chuckled. "Thank you. I've been very excited to meet you, Taylor. You have earned quite the reputation on my forum and through the challenges."

Taylor lost focus. Was this good or bad?

A strained smile crossed her mother's face. Her mom's concern spread to Taylor causing her to fear she had earned a poor reputation with Professor Davis.

"It's an exciting time for Taylor, and I'm sure you both are very proud of her to make it this far in the process." She pointed to three chairs in front of her desk as she walked around her small desk and sat in her chair. "I trust your trip from England was good?"

Taking a seat, Taylor nodded. "Yes, it was a good trip. We arrived two days ago and have been adjusting to the time change…" Taylor trailed off as she noticed a complex ruler sitting on Professor Davis' desk. "Do you mind if I take a quick photo of that ruler, Professor

Davis?"

Professor Davis chuckled. "You're a photographer?"

"Oh, no. If I see something I don't recognize or know its purpose, I take a photo and look it up later."

"You can take a photo. It's a slide rule. The predecessor to the electronic calculator."

Taylor looked at the wooden ruler-like device, unsure how it performed any calculation.

Professor Davis leaned back in her chair and said, "I assume you have worked out the financials of attending MIT?"

Tiny alarms sounded inside Taylor's head. "Not fully." Her eyes dropped as the words came out.

Professor Davis gave no sign of surprise. She had a championship poker face.

Taylor's mom spoke up. "We have discussed the financials. Loans are out of the question. We have told Taylor it makes little sense to accumulate debt to attend MIT when she has offers of full scholarships to three of the top universities back home."

"Wow, three full scholarships. That's great, Taylor! I'm partial to MIT, but I can't argue against what your mom says. If I were in her shoes, I would have the same concerns about my child going into debt at such a young age."

Taylor's dad nodded. "It's definitely not an easy decision."

"Professor Davis," Taylor interrupted, "if I don't receive a last-dollar scholarship from your coding competition, I won't be able to afford MIT."

Professor Davis sat quietly, rubbing her chin. "Let me check something," she said, taking a brief moment to consult her tablet. "I see you qualified for several scholarships, which will cover about half of the cost."

"That's correct. And if I win your competition, the prize money will cover the rest. But if I don't win, I'm not sure what else to do." Taylor was looking to Professor Davis for suggestions. "I've had awful luck when applying for other scholarships."

Professor Davis sat quietly for a moment. "Taylor, we do have a full scholarship in electrical engineering available."

"Electrical engineering?" That's definitely in my area of interest, but it's not my passion. Taylor looked at her parents and then back to Professor Davis. "How would a degree path in electrical engineering affect my future in artificial intelligence?"

"Well, you wouldn't be able to obtain an emphasis in AI. However, if everything worked out, you could apply for graduate school and pursue AI then. A lot of students take similar paths."

"You mean wait four years?" Taylor did the math in her head not liking how the numbers worked out. She looked at the slide rule and wondered if it would give her a different answer. "But that means I would be 18 by the time I get to dabble in anything AI."

"Don't look at it that way, Taylor." Professor Davis tapped the tips of her fingers together. "You would obtain an undergraduate degree related to computer science and be debt free. Because of your young age, you would have your bachelor's degree at the same age as most of our entering freshmen. That's quite an accomplishment. Assuming you perform well, you would have a chance for a full scholarship to graduate school."

"It is a great offer, and I like electronics and gadgets. It's just — "

"I realize the electrical engineering scholarship came out of nowhere. I'm just offering you a guaranteed path to get on campus." Professor Davis adjusted her glasses. "You have so much going for you, and I don't want you putting so much stress on yourself to do well on the coding competition. You know so much stress is not conducive to an optimal outcome."

Taylor didn't know what to say. She came here to get Professor Davis' approval of her ability to attend college and win the competition. But, a degree in electrical engineering? It just wouldn't be the same as diving right into AI.

"Don't allow the competition to occupy your every thought while you're on campus. You have performed remarkably well over the past year, but Saturday will be entirely different. Strange place, a room full of people, and the hardest challenge I've ever given." Professor Davis raised her tablet off the desk. "Your test scores are near perfect, but as you know, I don't award scholarships by test scores alone. I prefer my coding challenges. I get to see what each person is made of. Not only over time but also under pressure when it matters most." She tapped her tablet a few times and then looked up at Taylor. "You improved your standing with each challenge against people four years older. Remarkable if I say so myself. In fact, your ability to assess a problem, recognize patterns and make a quick decision is remarkable." Raising her eyebrows, she looked squarely at Taylor. "Did you know that you finish the challenges faster than the average participant? That's another strength you have working in your favor."

"How can I be faster when I am struggling to finish? I would have guessed I was slower than almost everyone," Taylor said.

"Who said everyone completes my coding challenges? You are in a very small minority of people who have successfully completed each challenge."

Only a few of us finish the challenges? Taylor sat back in her chair, letting the words sink in. "I don't know what to say to that. I almost can't believe it." Taylor shifted in her seat, suddenly uncomfortable. *If I am as good and as smart as she says I am, then why does everything feel so hard all the time?*

"Decisions like these shouldn't be taken lightly, but we are up against Father Time," Professor Davis said. "Take a few minutes and think it over. If you turn the electrical engineering scholarship down, I'll offer it to another prospective student this weekend. It's entirely up to you."

Taylor closed her eyes to gather her thoughts. *What would Hamburglar do? He'd probably tell me not to give up on my dream.*

Her mom put a hand on Taylor's shoulder. "It's an excellent offer." She looked at her husband.

"Yes, Taylor," her dad said. "You should consider this generous offer. It solves a lot of problems."

Taylor opened her eyes and looked at her parents for a brief moment. She turned back to Professor Davis. "I don't need that long to decide. I'm sorry, but I can't accept your offer."

Professor Davis stood and studied Taylor. "Are you sure? I want you to give it serious consideration."

Taylor shrugged her shoulders. "Electrical

engineering isn't for me. I'll take my chances in the competition."

Her dad rubbed his temple. Her mom's head dropped. Taylor started to doubt her decision, but she wasn't going back on it now.

"Well, in that case, I look forward to seeing you at the mixer tomorrow night and at the competition the day after. Good luck, Miss Hart. I hope you are successful."

"Thank you," Taylor said, hoping she made the right decision.

Taylor's parents stood and shook Professor Davis' hand. "If Taylor enters MIT this coming fall, does the school have any experience with students so young?" her dad asked.

"Yes, we do. This year we have the possibility of two young students, which makes it a special year. Taylor is just a few months older and in computer science, just like the other student. I'm sure you'll meet at the mixer." Professor Davis gestured everyone toward the door.

Taylor turned to her dad and spoke in Mandarin as they left the office, asking if he thought the other young student was from England, too. He laughed and followed her through the door.

7

Professor Baker

Aiden was in the Hayden Memorial Library working steadily to finish his project. His meeting with Professor Davis that morning reenergized him. Even after he tidied up a few areas of code, he was still having trouble with a critical section and couldn't find the root cause. Pulling up the message forum, Aiden typed a message.

Vesuvius, I need some help finding a problem in my code. I hate to ask because I know you are busy with the coding competition this weekend, but can you take a quick look at it and see if anything sticks out? Link attached. - Hamburglar

Aiden stood up and walked around to stretch his legs. Think Aiden. Think. The disk memory cache must be connected in some way. CIRE must have access to — . Aiden noticed a group of students gathering in the southeast corner of the library. "I wonder what that's all about?"

Not realizing he had spoken the words aloud, a male voice behind Aiden responded. "It's a Campus Preview Weekend activity."

Aiden's head swiveled around in the direction of the voice. "Thanks. I didn't see you there." A college age boy was standing near him. "How do you know?"

"You're welcome, and it's easy to spot activities this weekend. That's Professor Olivia Baker, so it's probably a talk about physics."

Aiden considered the name and looked at Professor Baker, thinking she looked like his mom's friend from college.

"Everyone tries to avoid her classes."

Aiden was curious why so many students would show up for an event led by a teacher with that kind of reputation.

Professor Baker stood in front of the small group as she spoke. She had curly, dark hair. She was short with an athletic build. Aiden noticed her stance made her appear ready to run a marathon at a moment's notice. She wore tennis shoes with her business dress and thought she might indeed be able to run a marathon.

Aiden was drawn in immediately upon hearing the subject of the talk. Quantum computing was both the future and the holy grail of computer science. Thirty minutes had passed before Professor Baker concluded. Aiden applauded and a few others joined in, but most students just scattered to their next planned activity.

Although everyone else had disappeared, curiosity got the better of him, and Aiden made his way toward Professor Baker. It was just he and Professor Baker remaining. Wow. They didn't waste any time leaving.

"Professor, if you have a minute, I would like to ask you a few questions."

"Of course, ask your questions. Also, thank you for the applause. I don't get that often." Professor Baker straightened a stack of papers she was holding. "What are your questions?"

"You mentioned once a working quantum computer is established, it could be used to crack anything protected on classical computers. What is the big hurdle keeping such a computer from being made today?"

She stopped rustling through her papers after hearing his question. "Quantum error correction is the field holding up the next step forward. I couldn't say what will hold us back after that."

"Any guesses how many years until that problem is solved?"

"Some believe we will never overcome error correction in quantum computing. I believe quantum supremacy will happen at some point, but it won't happen without better error detection." She smiled and extended her hand. "I'm sorry. I didn't get your name."

Aiden reached out and shook the professor's hand. "Aiden. I'm here for Campus Preview Weekend and caught your talk by pure luck. I'm glad I did. It was very interesting!" Aiden stopped himself from sounding too excited.

"Thank you, Aiden." Professor Baker said. "I am glad you enjoyed the talk. What major will you be pursuing?"

Aiden placed his hands in his pockets as he answered. "Computer science and physics."

Professor Baker's eyes narrowed. "Ah, the incoming freshman with the dual major request. We don't see that every day. What did you say your last name was?"

Aiden shifted his weight between each foot and looked at the ground. "I didn't. Anders. Aiden Anders."

She took a step back and studied Aiden. An awkward silence settled between them.

"Aiden, there you are," his mom said.

The voice of his mom breaking the silence caught him off guard, and Aiden jumped back and tripped over a nearby chair. He hit the floor and let out a small grunt. "That didn't feel good."

Aiden's dad helped him up.

His mom stood looking at Olivia Baker. Her hand

went to her throat and fiddled with the necklace she wore.

"Mom, this is Professor Baker. Professor Baker, my parents," Aiden said with a big smile.

"Olivia. It's been a long time. How are you?" Aiden's mom asked.

Aiden cleared his throat. "You two know each other?"

"It's Professor Baker now." Her eyes focused on the necklace Aiden's mom was clutching. "Of all the places to meet. I thought I was imagining things when I saw you in Professor Davis' office yesterday. But no, here you are." Professor Baker's expression turned cold. "If you will excuse me, I have another activity I must attend in the Hill Building." She abruptly turned and walked off.

Aiden's face crinkled. "That was the Olivia Baker from your yearbook? Your old friend from school?"

Aiden's mom turned to his dad. "Well, that could've gone better."

Still looking at his dad, his mom answered, "Yes, Aiden. That's her." She turned to Aiden and motioned for him to take a seat at the table nearest them.

"What happened? You get along with everyone." Aiden asked. What is the point of having friends if this is how it turns out?

His mom sat down next to Aiden and adjusted her posture. "We became fast friends in our first semester at college. Both of us were away from home for the first time. We crossed paths in freshman orientation. It feels like a lifetime ago." She gripped her necklace, and her eyes had an unfocused look to them. "Olivia gave me this necklace as a gift before our falling out."

"Tell him the story. He needs to know what happened since she may be his teacher one day," Aiden's dad said.

"Mom, did you steal dad away from Professor Baker?"

She laughed. "No. Not at all."

"It's much worse than that," his dad said.

"To Olivia," Aiden's mom waved her hand in the air, "it would be one hundred times worse. We had a falling out over our final project in computer science. It was a group project, and we were partners. The night before the project was due, someone spilled coffee on the computer we were using."

Aiden was leaning on the edge of his seat. "You didn't have a backup?"

"Yes, but it was several days old, and we couldn't recreate the lost work in time. We both made our only Bs in undergrad because of it. She was distraught and blew up. She blamed me for tarnishing her academic record and going into school loan debt because she missed out on a scholarship for graduate school."

"That's exactly why I usually prefer to work alone on my projects. If something goes wrong, it's no one's fault but mine." Aiden looked at his mom. "So, you spilled the coffee? I didn't even know you liked coffee."

Aiden's mom exhaled a slow, deep breath. "I don't know who spilled the coffee. I told her I wasn't the one responsible, but Olivia thought otherwise." She rubbed the back of her neck. "It doesn't even matter who spilled the coffee. It seems she still hasn't put the past behind her."

His dad spoke up. "I think Professor Baker may be harder on you than a normal student because of her grudge against your mom."

"I see. Do you think I should try to avoid her classes?" Aiden didn't have that kind of time or patience. "I can't imagine why she would hold it against me. I wasn't even born then. Besides, a lot can change in a few years. Don't teachers have a code of ethics or something?"

"Teaching at MIT was Olivia's dream from day one," Aiden's mom said. "I didn't expect her to have that kind of reaction to us meeting so many years later. Your dad's right to believe you may have problems if you have her as a teacher. It was a lot more complicated and emotional than my abridged version of the story."

"She's only one teacher." He looked at his dad. "How bad could it be?"

"We shouldn't ignore that ever since you pursued

this dual major, it's been one speed bump after another, and you keep ignoring them," his dad said. "Sometimes it serves us well to pay attention to the signs life gives us."

"I'm not ignoring any of the speed bumps, dad. They're just risks I'm willing to take if it means being one of the first people on Mars." Aiden looked at his mom. "I have just one question. Why do you still wear that necklace if you and Professor Baker aren't even friends?"

"To remind myself the importance of friendship," his mom said as she stared off into the distance.

8

Playing Hooky

Aiden sat at the table in their hotel room, working on his project. It was late on Friday afternoon, and the mixer started in thirty minutes. Social situations were something he avoided whenever possible. However, this mixer was different. He looked forward to meeting Vesuvius for the first time, and he wanted to show Professor Davis he could socialize with others. It was a small price to pay if it meant getting his dual major request approved.

A chime sounded on his computer. He looked to the top of the browser tab and saw he had a new message on Professor Davis' forum. He clicked on the tab and there, staring him in the face, was a message from Vesuvius with a one-word subject line. Fixed.

Yeah, baby! Aiden opened the message and began reading.

Fixed the cache. See you at the mixer? I'll be

wearing an MIT shirt. - V

Aiden downloaded the file attachment and looked over Vesuvius' comments and corrected code. "That's it! Vesuvius found the problem like it was the most obvious thing ever."

Aiden corrected the code and ran several quality checks on his datasets to make sure everything was okay.

He replied to Vesuvius's message. Vesuvius, this is more than I expected. Thank you! I must show you my project and what I am doing soon. It's cool. See you at the mixer. Looking forward to meeting you in person. - Hamburglar

Aiden let out a sigh and reluctantly stood from his chair. "Mom. Dad. I'm headed to the mixer." He would finally meet Vesuvius. Plus, maybe he'd get to meet the other 14-year-old incoming freshman while he was there, too.

Walking through campus was a little weird for Aiden. The general terrain was flat, and the grass was neatly trimmed. Back home, he was surrounded by tall ridges, which formed valleys that stretched for miles. He pulled out the pamphlet for the mixer, getting his bearings. Being sure he had found the building where the mixer was taking place, he watched as the students entered. He noticed a majority of the students were wearing MIT shirts.

He looked down and noticed he was wearing one of his favorite shirts. "Nothing says thirteen like a turtle saying 'Cowabunga Dude' on your shirt." Would Vesuvius care about his age? His body temperature increased and his palms felt sweaty.

Aiden heard footsteps approaching behind him, then he heard a boy's voice.

"Hey, there. I couldn't help but notice your shoes," the guy with a red jacket said. He was a tall, imposing figure of a teenager.

"Thanks. Um, nice jacket."

"Have any chewie on ya?" the boy asked.

"I'm sorry?"

"Americans call it chewing gum."

"Yeah. I have a few pieces left. Cotton Candy flavor. It's the best." Aiden handed him a piece of gum.

"Mind if I have two?"

Aiden looked in the package and noticed he only had one piece left. "Sure, I guess," Aiden responded as he handed over his last piece of gum. That was kind of rude.

"Thanks," said the teenager. He shoved the two pieces of gum into his mouth and smiled while his hand opened and released the gum wrappers.

"You dropped your gum wrappers." Aiden pointed at the ground where they had landed. His eyes moved over to the recycle and waste bins a few feet from them. "There's a trash can right there."

The teenager took a step closer to Aiden. "Are you on litter patrol or something?"

"No, but we all need to do our part. Don't you think?"

"Our part?" The teenager laughed and swept his hair back over his head. "Dude. If anything needs to be thrown in the trash, it's those shoes you're wearing." He took another step toward Aiden.

"What's your problem?" Aiden held up his hands.

"You're my problem. Why don't you mind your own business." The boy shoved Aiden with one arm.

Aiden was forced to take a few steps back to remain on his feet and even then he wasn't sure how he remained standing. He noticed several people were witnessing the exchange between him and the taller, older boy. "My shoes aren't the problem. Your attitude is." Aiden could feel his face heating up. He didn't enjoy attracting unwanted attention, and this was escalating past the point of a simple disagreement.

The older boy looked around at the crowd that had gathered. He took a step closer to exaggerate his height and size over Aiden. "Why don't you find your mommy and daddy before I call campus security and tell them a kid is lost and wandering around campus?" He popped his collar checking to make sure it stayed up. "This is a place for grown-ups." The boy slowly took a few steps backwards and then turned and walked away.

Aiden looked around and noticed that everyone was staring at him. Two guys approached and one asked, "Everything ok? Want us to call your parents?"

After some discussion and reassurance from Aiden, the two boys reluctantly went on about their business. Aiden slid the pamphlet out of his back pocket and looked at it again. He watched the guy in the red jacket walk into the mixer, and his mouth dropped open. The boy was going to Professor Davis' mixer.

Pressing a hand to his stomach to quell his nausea, he thought about walking into a room full of older kids. That idea made him feel worse than meeting up with the guy in the red jacket again.

Aiden crumpled up the pamphlet and discarded it in the recycle bin. He couldn't do it. Maybe it was better to stay friends with Vesuvius online only. At least that way, he might keep a friend for once. His eyes caught a schedule of events taped to the bin in front of him. Activities at Killian Court were scheduled around the clock for the entire weekend. Going back to his room now would raise red flags with his parents. They would expect him to explain why he returned early. If he did that, they would definitely pull the plug on him attending any college away from home. Killian Court was close by, and with no other obvious choices, it seemed as good a place as any to seek asylum.

Reaching Killian Court, Aiden sat down on a step. He watched families walking their dogs, children playing, and the many Campus Preview Weekend activities taking place.

Disappointed in himself for skipping out on the mixer, he began composing a message to Vesuvius explaining his absence. Aiden could hear his dad telling him, "Don't borrow trouble." When the time came, he would worry about explaining his absence to Professor Davis.

Explaining to Vesuvius why he missed the mixer proved to be harder than adapting CIRE for his presentation. He deleted his message, unhappy with both himself and his explanation. He slid his phone into his pocket and glanced at his watch. Only another two hours before the mixer ended and he could head back to his room without raising any suspicions from his parents. It was going to be a long night.

9

Mixer

Taylor noticed a flower not familiar to her as she walked to the mixer. Just another reminder how far Boston was from home. She bent down to take a closer look. It was beautiful with its delicate white petals and white center. She pulled out her phone to take a quick photo so she could look up what kind it was later.

When she arrived at the building holding the mixer, she saw students lined up outside. All at once she was quite nervous.

"I'll be outside right here in about three hours," Taylor said.

"Ok. We'll be here waiting for you then," her dad said.

Inhaling a deep breath, she released it and blended into the line of students and walked through the doors, immediately spotting Professor Davis.

"Taylor, it is good to see you," Professor Davis said. "I am glad you could make it this evening." She motioned for Taylor to follow her.

As Taylor followed Professor Davis, she looked around the large room, taking in the people. "Is everyone here taking part in the competition tomorrow?"

"No, not everyone. Most of the students here are in computer science, though there are a few prospective freshmen from other disciplines who make their way in throughout the night."

"I have to prove to my parents I can interact with older students."

Professor Davis pointed to several areas in the large room where the students were gathering. "Over there we have backgammon, chess, checkers, Monopoly, Blokus, and over here we have a rook tournament about to start. Don't worry, I'm sure some other games will emerge before the night is over."

Taylor nodded. Suddenly, she was very aware of how much older all the other kids were.

"We also have snacks and drinks on the table over by the double doors." Professor Davis looked at Taylor. "Is there a game you like to play, Taylor?"

Shrugging, Taylor looked at Professor Davis. "I thought I would play chess." The thought of dealing with the stress that came with meeting older kids and trying to fit in was almost too much. Better to keep things low-key.

"Nonsense," Professor Davis said, shaking her head. "You came here to socialize and make the most of your night. I would suggest you make your way over to the Blokus area and find a partner."

"Uh," Taylor said as she pulled and twisted at her watch. "Is Blokus an American thing?"

"Not at all. French, actually."

"Who from the forum is here?"

"Quite a few. DRIVOVR, 2CL4SCL, 5LTRETR, Sarek, and plenty of others."

"Hamburglar?" Taylor asked.

"No, not yet, I'm afraid. Oh, my. There's the pizza delivery. Excuse me, dear." Professor Davis waved her arms to get the young lady's attention.

Taylor hummed to calm her nerves and headed toward the Blokus game. On her way, she stopped in front of the snack table and grabbed a cup of lemonade. Looking proudly at the cup filled with American lemonade, she smiled. Lemonade from America was something she had heard about from classmates back home. She had been waiting all weekend to try it.

As she lifted the cup to take a drink, someone bumped her from the side, and she spilled her lemonade down the front of her shirt and jeans.

"Watch yourself, buddy. There's plenty of room

here without you bumping into everyone and causing problems," she heard a girl on the other side of the snack table say to an older boy in a bright red jacket.

Taylor looked down at her clothes. "Great."

"I'm not the one with a problem," the boy said, looking down at Taylor and her spilled lemonade.

The boy stood about six feet tall with dark brown hair that was not quite shoulder length. He had the mannerisms and build of a surfer. His light brown skin was smooth, and high cheekbones framed his light brown eyes.

"I'm not the one wearing my drink on my shirt." The boy stood there and laughed, his tall figure towering over Taylor and the other girl. "Maybe you should have your parents come and get your little sister." He huffed and walked away.

The girl turned to Taylor. "I'm sorry! Let me help you get cleaned up," she said.

"It's ok. I can just go back to my room and — "

"Whoa. Stop right there. Don't let that jerk and a little spilled lemonade ruin your evening. If you go back to your room now, you'll miss all the fun! This is a party." The girl motioned around the room with her arms. She then erupted in contagious laughter. "Maybe not the most exciting party you've ever seen, but a party none-the-less."

"Can I have a napkin to dry off?"

"Sure thing. Just promise not to hold our first encounter against me. By the way, I'm Morgan. You know me by," Morgan paused, bringing both feet together and holding up her right hand showing the Vulcan salute, "Sarek, on the forum."

Taylor smiled. "I'm Taylor. Vesuvius on the forum."

They shook hands and Morgan said, "Well. I am in the company of a hero. I'm honored to shake," Morgan paused, looking down at Taylor's hand, "the lemonade-soaked hand of the only person to beat David Hill in a coding challenge."

Taylor blushed and looked down at her feet. "Thank you. I got lucky on that one."

"I just wish it had been sooner, so we didn't have to deal with his bragging for so long."

Taylor laughed. "Thank you, Morgan." She appreciated Morgan's kind words. "I assumed you were a boy since Sarek was Spock's father."

Morgan smiled and said, "I assumed the same thing about you! I also assumed you were a senior in high school." Morgan relaxed and put her right hand on her hip. "Actually, you do remind me of my little sister, who looks about your age. She's my best friend." Her hand dropped from her hip. "Now, let's get you dried off. You can be my partner in Blokus. Have you played before?"

"No."

"It's a fun game, but it takes a long time to get the hang of it. Even longer to be successful."

A minute later Taylor was standing beside Morgan in a group of people watching the Blokus games. Instead of watching the game rules closely, Taylor was only half paying attention. She looked around the room and wondered if Hamburglar had made it yet. I hope he doesn't care about my age. Morgan doesn't seem to mind, but that other boy sure did.

When the game ended, a young man with curly, shoulder-length hair and Harry Potter style glasses spoke up, "New game! Let's pick new teams." He motioned at Taylor and Morgan, "You guys showed up at the perfect time. Do you know how to play? Think you could go a full round?"

"No chance," Taylor said. Yikes. I didn't mean to say that out loud.

Morgan gave Taylor a reassuring smile. "She will partner up with me. I've been playing a while."

Taylor's inexperience was met with smiles from the students looking at her. I guess they believe we will be easy to beat. They're probably right.

Morgan turned and whispered to Taylor. "We can get you up and running pretty quickly. The rules are easy. It's the strategy part that's difficult. But, it takes time and experience to really hone your skills."

Three hours later, Taylor and Morgan were the center of attention.

"I thought Taylor said she didn't know how to play," came a voice from one of the young men who just lost the championship game.

"I didn't, and I don't think I play it very well at that. Morgan carried us through this evening," Taylor said matter-of-factly.

"I don't know about that Taylor," Morgan said slowly.

"I think everyone here just got hustled."

Morgan laughed and said, "Let's go find another game to crash. You're my secret weapon. How are you at card games?"

"Oh. I don't know. What time is it?" Taylor pulled out her phone, hoping to have a message from Hamburglar. *Where is he? Did he see me and decided he didn't want to be friends with a 14-year-old?* The thought was depressing. "I'm feeling kind of tired. And the coding competition is tomorrow. I need to rest up," she said, putting her phone back in her pocket.

Morgan noticed Taylor glance at her phone. "Just another hour, that's all I ask. I'm glad to have a new friend and don't want to let you go just yet. Stay a little longer and play a few more of the other games with me." Her lips pouted up. "Please?"

Taylor was tempted. "I truly want to stay. I really do — "

"Then stay," Morgan pleaded. "What if Professor Davis gives us the early scoop before tomorrow?"

Taylor's eyes rolled. "You'll be just fine without me. It really has been a fun evening."

Several more people pleaded with her to stay and told her to live a little.

"My parents are waiting for me outside. I have to go." Taylor waved and headed toward the front door. Once outside the building, she paused, and a growing smile appeared on her face. The mixer had gone well, and she was happy she had met Morgan and made a new friend. But where was Hamburglar? Her smile faded as she walked outside to find her parents.

10

Sign In

Standing outside Building 32, Taylor was in awe of the architecture. The typical parallel lines and perpendicular intersections were nowhere to be found. "Wow. This is more incredible in person than I could have imagined. Have either of you ever seen a building that looked like a liquefied mirror?" she asked.

Taylor's dad stood beside her, looking up at the building with the same expression of wonder. "Can't say that I have. It's breathtaking. I can't imagine how long it took to build."

Once inside, Taylor was even more impressed. From the large square columns to the finished floor, she could not ignore the extensive use of concrete in the design and construction.

Taylor took in the spacious room around her. She saw a large group of teenagers congregating around a table where a young man held a clipboard. "Mom, dad, I need to get signed in for the competition. Don't forget it's four hours long, so be back at two." Taylor gave her parents a reassuring smile and waved them back toward the front entrance.

Her mom gave her a long and serious look. "Don't forget, your dad and I are just a phone call away." A tear welled up in the corner of her mom's eye. "I guess this is where I have to get used to the idea you won't always need us around."

Taylor's dad leaned in toward her. "Don't forget our deal. The outcome of this competition decides your future." He gave her a kiss on the forehead.

"We are so proud of you for making it this far," her mom said as she planted a kiss on Taylor's forehead.

Taylor smiled and hugged both of her parents. She continued to smile as she watched them walk out the front door.

While waiting in the sign in line, Taylor pulled out her phone to see if she had a message from Hamburglar. She was hoping there was some reasonable explanation for his absence at the mixer last night. Maybe he just got bogged down preparing for his panel presentation today. Or maybe he saw me and doesn't want to be friends with a little girl. Taylor opened her messages and saw a message from David Hill. "Could this morning get any worse?"

Vesuvius. You won't be as lucky as you were in the last challenge. Absolute fluke you won. I look forward to beating you in person. -David Hill

She took a deep breath and closed her eyes. Ugh! How could I have forgotten that David Hill would be here in person? "Focus. Just sign in, keep your head down, and do your best."

As Taylor moved along the line and approached the sign in table, she angled her body away from the group of students who had already picked up their name tags. She recognized a few of them from Professor Davis' mixer, but they paid her no attention.

Taylor looked at the young man standing behind the table. "Hi. Is this the sign in for the coding competition?"

The young man at the table allowed a small laugh to escape. "Hi, I'm Logan. Yes, it is. But it's only for incoming freshmen who qualified over the past year through Professor Davis' coding challenges." He pointed toward the corner of the room. "You can find the campus weekend tour group over there every thirty minutes."

"Uh, no. I need to sign in for the competition," Taylor said.

Logan stood still, waiting for her to move. After a few awkward seconds, he looked down at the table and then back up at Taylor.

"I'm on the list," she said.

Logan picked up his clipboard with a snap. "Name?"

"Taylor Hart," she said in a low voice.

Logan looked at her and stuttered, "I-I-I'm so so sorry, Taylor. I didn't expect someone so — so young to be competing. Please don't take any offense. Here. Here's your name tag."

Taylor thanked him and took the name tag. She noted both her real and forum names were listed. As she was sticking the name tag to the front of her shirt, she felt a tap on her shoulder. She turned around and saw the guy in the red jacket who had spilled her lemonade at the mixer. "Sorry," she said. "I'm not in line anymore. You can go ahead."

"Ah, the great and powerful Vesuvius. I've been looking forward to meeting you. Did you get my message this morning?"

The realization hit her like a bucket of cold water. "You must be David Hill," she said, crossing her arms.

"The one and only." David smiled and stroked his hair with his hand.

Taylor rolled her eyes. Jerk. She looked around and noticed the other students were all listening and watching. Anger raced through Taylor. "Everyone around you can smell your insecurity."

David Hill threw back his head and laughed. He grabbed the clipboard from Logan. "Hey man, are you sure you didn't make a mistake? Did you check her photo ID to make sure she is who she says she is?" He laughed again. "Oh wait, they don't even give photo ID's to babies. My bad." He threw the clipboard down on the table and kept his eyes on Taylor.

"I assure you, David. You will discover that my name being on that list is no mistake." She turned around to walk away but ran right into Morgan instead.

David smiled as he looked at Morgan. "Oh, finally. Vesuvius' babysitter is here."

"Something smelled rotten and my nose led me to you." Morgan stood her ground.

"Thank you, thank you, thank you, Morgan!" David pointed his finger in Taylor's face. "Mommy and daddy won't be here to help you get your coding right. You're on your own today, Vesuvius."

"Beat it, David," Morgan said. "Leave before I lose my patience, and you find your expertly dry-cleaned jacket stained from the soles of my shoes."

Taylor gulped and stepped closer to steer Morgan away and toward the room.

David Hill raised his hands in a mock gesture of surrender and started walking away.

Taylor turned to Morgan and said, "How did you

do that?"

"Don't pay him any attention. He's a jerk and just trying to intimidate you." Morgan smiled. "The more pompous they are, the easier they are to scare off."

"He irritates me like few people can." Taylor sighed and brushed her hair out of her eyes.

"David's just mad someone beat him. I bet when he realized you were a girl and much younger than him, it was more than his ego could stand." Morgan directed a long, cold stare in David Hill's direction. "Don't worry," she said, "no one likes him."

"Hamburglar asked me to beat David Hill today during the competition. Even if it's not me, I just hope someone does."

"Hamburglar? He's cool. You two have worked on some killer projects over the past year. I always love seeing what you two are up to together. What's he like outside the forum?

"I couldn't tell you. I was hoping we'd meet last night, but he never showed up." Taylor saw the other students entering the lab and checked her watch. "I think we better go find a seat."

11

One Winner

Taylor followed Morgan into the computer lab and found an open workstation. She grabbed a seat next to Morgan. Relax. You've got this. All you need is a top three finish.

Pushing David Hill from her thoughts, she arranged her pen and a pad of paper on the side of her desk. Taylor turned her notebook over so Hello Kitty on the front cover wouldn't show. Her face turned red hoping no one else saw her notebook cover. The last thing she needed was another reason for David Hill to make fun of her. She pulled up her favorite playlist on her phone, connected her headphones, and took another deep breath.

She felt the desk rattle as someone moved the chair in the workstation opposite hers. She looked up and felt the blood drain from her face. No, no, no, no! Peering over the partition that separated her desk from the other was David Hill. This cannot be happening.

"Well, well. You look surprised to see me. Don't worry. I'll just be here making sure you don't receive any outside help from mommy and daddy this time," David Hill said loud enough so the entire lab could hear. He stood there with a crooked smirk on his face, waiting for her reaction.

A few students were whispering to each other and looking in Taylor's general direction. When she didn't respond, David Hill laughed and sat down at his desk.

Morgan placed her hand on Taylor's elbow. "Don't pay him any attention."

"I knew I would probably be the youngest person here today, but I never imagined David Hill would be such a jerk in person too. I thought internet bullying stayed on the internet. I see I was wrong."

Professor Davis walked through the door and greeted the room. "Good morning! Did anyone have any trouble getting through the crowd? The MIT Better World Campaign had Senator Matthew Jones speaking, which made campus very crowded this morning." Professor Davis looked around the room. A couple of the students shook their heads, but most sat there in silence. "Good, I'm glad none of you had any trouble this morning. I trust everyone knows how to power on the computer in front of you." Lots of good-natured laughs filled the room in response to her humorous attempt to put everyone at ease.

David Hill responded. "Everyone over the age of fourteen does, Professor." He craned his neck so his eyes caught Taylor's gaze over the partition.

Taylor glared at David Hill. "Are you scared of being beaten again by a fourteen-year-old girl?" She took one deep breath after another, willing herself to remain in her seat.

Professor Davis' smile faded. "Remind me of your name again, sir?"

"David Hill."

"That's right, Mr. Hill. How could I forget one of the top incoming freshmen? Especially when you and your parents were just in my office earlier this morning, and I explicitly told you to be on your best behavior during this competition if you want to attend MIT this fall."

David's face flushed red as he squirmed in his seat.

Taylor allowed a small smile to escape.

Professor Davis said, "Before we get started, I want to talk a bit about conduct and this scholarship." She paced across the floor before looking back at the class. "I wonder. Should the cumulative actions of one person affect the entire group?"

Morgan's hand went up.

"Yes, Sarek," Professor Davis said, making it clear she knew everyone's pseudonym on her forum.

"I don't think it should," Morgan responded.

A young man spoke up behind Taylor. "His family's legacy on campus will protect him."

Is he talking about David Hill? Taylor waited in silence with the rest of the students as Professor Davis continued to pace in front of the room.

"His family's legacy at MIT will not protect him in this competition," Professor Davis said.

David Hill stood from his seat and all eyes were focused on him. "I think I should have a say in this, Professor. So what if my great grandfather has a building on campus? Big deal."

"Mr. Hill, we have heard quite enough from you this morning. Please take a seat and don't speak again unless I recognize you," Professor Davis said tersely.

Taylor couldn't help but smile as David Hill plopped down into his chair, arms crossed over his chest like an angry child who just got his toy taken away.

Professor Davis cleared her throat and continued, "As you know, every year I prepare multiple challenges for this competition." She held up her right hand with a yellow sheet of paper in it. "This was the challenge I had planned to give — the one I was prepared to hand out to everyone competing. However," she said as she threw the papers into the recycle bin, "recent events have changed my mind."

Taylor leaned forward in her seat, hanging on every

word. This was it. Maybe Professor Davis would announce that more people could win. She hoped there would be more than three winners this year. More scholarship spots means more opportunities for me to get one. Her heart fluttered with the prospect. Professor Davis held up her left hand, holding a white piece of paper. "Thanks to Mr. Hill's behavior, I have decided this challenge can only have one winner."

A collective groan filled the room. Several hands shot into the air, and students started mumbling to their neighbors. Angry faces glared across the classroom toward David Hill. Taylor leaned back in her chair. This can't be happening! The odds of beating David Hill two challenges in a row seemed impossible. Winning the last challenge still felt like a fluke.

"Please everyone. Quiet down." Professor Davis held up both hands to quiet the room. "Some people have to learn the hard way, and I want this to be a lesson to all of you." She paced the floor for a few seconds before continuing. "Miss Hart, you have been the most frequent recipient of Mr. Hill's outbursts and bullying over the past year, and it has not gone unnoticed by me. Miss Hart, you will decide whether David Hill is disqualified." Professor Davis turned and walked out of the room.

Choose David Hill's fate in this competition? Sure, I want revenge, but not like this. She looked at Morgan and then around at the other students.

"You can't be serious!" David Hill yelled, as Professor Davis vanished through the door. "I've earned this."

Taylor sat frozen, gripping the sides of her chair. She felt paralyzed, like she couldn't make herself move. If she disqualified him from the competition, she would be an instant hero. The silence from the other students begged her to disqualify him.

Morgan looked at Taylor. Her eyes jumped between Taylor and David Hill. Shaking her head, she whispered, "I wouldn't blame you if you tossed him. No one would."

Kicking him out of the competition? That seems wrong, even for David Hill. What he said was true. He deserves to be here — he has earned it just like everyone else.

She took a deep breath and stood up. "David Hill should remain in the competition," she said.

Audible gasps came from all directions. Morgan covered her face with her hands and mumbled something in what sounded like Klingon.

Taylor's pulse quickened, and she could hear her heartbeat in her ears. It was not a popular decision, but she felt she had made the right call. The coding competition would end today with no one being able to say she skewed the odds in her favor.

David Hill smiled and laughed.

Taylor sat back down, surprised by his smug reaction. Ignoring her need for a scholarship, she now had one goal. Beat David Hill.

Two people entered the room, casting suspicious looks over the room in Professor Davis' absence. One of them walked to the whiteboard. "Follow this link, and your challenge question will appear. It has ten parts and revolves around shape recognition. Many major industries find this problem's solution vital to their success. Today, it is vital to your success. You have four hours starting now. Good luck." He wrote the time on the whiteboard. 10:07.

Taylor immediately typed the URL and read over the problem. She was not thrilled with the challenge, but she believed she could finish within the four-hour time limit. The problem was similar to a challenge she had done well on over the summer. Slipping on her headphones, she started her favorite playlist and mentally began to organize her plan of attack.

12

32-144

Aiden stopped in front of room 32-144, one of two flat classrooms on the floor. Wearing his well-worn backpack, he stood with a thumb under each shoulder strap and waited. Beside him stood his luggage with NASA Space Camp patches sewn on, packed with four additional notebook computers and their cables. The clock on the hallway wall read nine thirty. That gave him forty-five minutes before his presentation was due to begin.

He peeked inside the room and saw rows of seats arranged in a half-circle in front of a stage, with a small table in the front for the panel of judges and a table on stage for him. "Looks like I found the correct room."

He made his way to the front of the classroom and pulled the computers and cabling from his luggage. He booted up each computer and plugged them into the electrical power strip underneath the table. Once he had everything connected, he turned the main computer's display toward the small table in front where the panel would be sitting.

He ran through two project scenarios. "Awesome. Everything is running perfect." He pumped his fist. "If you will just run that way for the panel, I won't have anything to worry about."

With ten minutes until the presentation, he pulled up a project he and Vesuvius had been working on together. It was their attempt at creating artificial intelligence to carry on a conversation with a human.

"Chatbot, how are your operations?"

A few seconds of silence passed. "Fine," Chatbot said.

"Skipping last night's mixer was a mistake. I missed out on meeting Vesuvius."

"I admit that doesn't sound good."

"Good morning, Mr. Anders. Are you ready?" Professor Davis was standing just inside the double door entrance to the room.

Aiden's head jerked in the direction of the voice. "Oh. Hey there, Professor Davis." He took a step back from the table and wiped his hands on his pants. "Yeah, everything should be ready. Sorry, I didn't hear you come in."

She walked toward the front of the room. "I

expect big things from you today since you skipped out on the mixer last night. But I'm sure you have a good reason why you missed it..." she trailed off. The serious look on her face told Aiden that she was not at all happy with him.

Aiden lowered his head. "I'm sorry, Professor. I don't really have a good excuse." Aiden stuffed his hands in his pockets. "Did the coding competition already begin?"

"It just started a few minutes ago. There will only be one winner this year," she sighed.

"One winner?" he asked, sounding alarmed. "Vesuvius is counting on the competition scholarship to go here."

"It's unfortunate. But, it will work itself out in a few hours. No need to get all worked up about it." She clasped her hands together. "So, who, or what," she looked around the room, "were you talking to when I walked in?"

"Uh," Aiden said as he turned to look at the table, "Vesuvius and I have been working on a chatbot. It's in its early phase, and I was just passing the time until someone showed up."

"I see." She looked from the computer screen to Aiden. "Vesuvius," she said. "You and Vesuvius have been working on this project together?"

"Yeah. It's been a long time in the making."

Professor Davis bent down and adjusted her bright

pink socks where they met her sneakers. "You two have created some impressive work over the past year."

Aiden looked at her socks and realized his Crocs had finally met their match. "Vesuvius is the best coder I know."

Professor Davis looked at Aiden over the top of her pink-framed glasses and gave him an odd smile. "Vesuvius was at the mixer last night and appeared to have a great time mingling with the other students."

Aiden felt a little queasy in his stomach. Did I just lose my only friend? "That's great," he muttered.

Professor Davis cleared her throat and pointed to the computers on the table. "Enough about that. Mr. Anders, I would like to see the project you had pulled up when I walked into the room."

"Huh?" Aiden cleared his throat. "It's not just my work and not what I prepared to present to the panel today."

"When I walked into the room this morning, you were having a conversation with this computer. That seems impressive to me."

"Yeah, I guess," Aiden interjected. "We call it Chatbot. Our goal is to have a conversation with Chatbot and not realize it's artificial. It's just that," Aiden looked at Professor Davis, "I feel I should ask Vesuvius for permission to share it since it's a joint effort. I don't think he would mind, but I should get his permission first." Plus, I don't want to make things any worse between us than they already are.

Professor Davis smiled and considered Aiden for a moment. "I hardly think he would mind," she said and chuckled.

Aiden took a step backwards, waving his hands. "But it's still in development, very early development."

"Well, none of the professors here today will expect your project to be perfect. We only have a limited amount of time, so you'll need to decide if you want to show us Chatbot." Professor Davis glanced at her watch and then looked back toward both entrances to the classroom. "We have three and a half hours before I need to head back to the coding competition. And speaking of time, the other two professors are late."

Aiden studied the computers set up on the table. His dual major request depended on this presentation, and Professor Davis was asking him to present on an entirely different project. The slide deck, index cards, and presentation booklets he brought with him would be worthless. If he showed Chatbot, he would have to do the entire presentation unrehearsed. Chatbot was very impressive when it cooperated, but it didn't have anything to do with radio astronomy. He tapped his fist into his palm a few times.

Professor Davis continued, "If you want to be a part of the first team on Mars, then you must learn how to work well in a team environment. A single person won't improve artificial intelligence. It takes a team, and this would be good practice for you getting accustomed to last minute changes to the schedule."

"I know, and I have worked well with Vesuvius. I just feel I should present my own work. Plus, you told me my project had to combine radio astronomy and computer science."

"You got me there." She smiled and rubbed her chin.

"Maybe Vesuvius and I could present Chatbot to you when we get to campus this fall? We'll have more work done by then."

"We'll talk more about this later. Which project are you more passionate about? Chatbot or the one you came prepared to present?"

"Chatbot. CIRE has a lot of potential to change the world, but Chatbot is my favorite."

Professor Davis took a drink from her cup before speaking. Aiden noticed the gigantic crazy straw she used. "I'll admit I wanted to test your reaction and try to understand just what goes on in that brain of yours."

13

Panel Decision

Aiden heard the double doors open, and someone said, "Professor Davis! Don't start without us! We've been waiting in 32-124." Two people made their way to the front of the room. "Sorry, I couldn't read your handwriting."

"Do either of you need coffee or tea before we begin?"

Both of them held up cardboard cups with white lids and shook their heads.

"Mr. Anders, I would like you to meet Professors Deskins and Baker."

Aiden stared at the two professors as they walked toward the front of the room.

Professor Deskins extended his hand. "It's nice to meet you. Professor Davis speaks highly of you."

Aiden shook Professor Deskins' hand and glanced

at Professor Baker. Aiden gulped and adjusted his collar.

Seeing Professor Baker hesitate, Professor Davis jumped in and said, "And this is Professor Baker. She teaches in the physics department and specializes in radio astronomy."

Aiden's heart beat like a drum in his ears.

"Mr. Anders. Your presentation better be memorable if you want to succeed on this campus." Professor Baker did not offer to shake Aiden's hand. Instead, she immediately took a seat next to Professor Deskins.

Was that some kind of cryptic warning? Aiden noticed Professor Deskins raised his eyebrows at Professor Baker as she sat down.

"Uh. Yes," Aiden responded, "I take my request for a dual major very seriously, and this project reflects the culmination of my efforts to attend MIT."

Professor Davis cleared her throat after looking between Aiden and Professor Baker. "Now then, Mr. Anders. The floor is yours. Go ahead and get started. We don't have any time to waste."

"Thank you. For my project, I will demonstrate the ability to analyze incoming radio data in real-time for signs of alien life."

Professor Deskins pointed to Aiden's computers on the table. "Is this like SETI?"

"I'm glad you asked," Aiden said. "Yes, it is. My project offers similar outcomes, but a different implementation searching for extraterrestrial intelligence. The data is analyzed live as it comes in from space telescopes, which eliminates the need for thousands upon thousands of volunteers and cuts the discovery time by twenty-two days, by my best estimate."

All three professors smiled, and Aiden felt he was beginning to hit his stride.

"SETI has been at this in some form since 1984, and you're saying you've bypassed the greater scientific community?" Professor Baker asked.

"I have laid the groundwork for something that has far more potential," Aiden said.

Professor Deskins glanced at the other two professors while nodding his head in approval.

"I will demonstrate that today." Aiden walked up to the main computer, which faced the panel. "I have two sets of data to present today, which I will load into CIRE so we can watch the analysis live. First, I will load a set of recorded data that contains unknown signals. It may be aliens or some other phenomena we don't yet understand." Aiden clicked on the start button. "If CIRE detects an artificial signal, it will alert us with a bright red screen."

The computer showed horizontal lines oscillating across the screen. Red, blue, and green data points danced around to visualize the incoming data. It looked like something out of a movie. Ninety-one seconds into the data stream, the screen turned red.

"There you have it. A warning showing it has detected something out of the norm."

"Mr. Anders, I fail to see the importance of this. SETI has essentially the same ability," Professor Baker said. "Over the timeline of the galaxy, weeks don't matter."

"This is instant and more efficient," Aiden interjected with a little more defensiveness in his tone than he would have liked. Breathe, Aiden. Breathe. You will not win her over by being rude. "With one modest computing cluster, signals like this could be analyzed using less power, while giving more accurate outcomes and resulting in less power usage. My project offers a centralized setup more suited for scientific research and adaptable to other fields."

Professor Baker leaned forward in her seat. "I need to review your code. This seems too good to be true. Will that be an issue?"

Aiden rubbed the back of his neck. He could feel the sweat rolling down his back and temple. Don't let her get to you. Going to Mars depends on this moment right here. "No, that won't be a problem, Professor Baker." Aiden took a deep breath. "Now, I'm loading the second set of recorded data, which contains no known artificial noise or signals. This data is from the Kepler-186 system using the Square Kilometer Array in Western Australia. Again, we can watch the data analysis as it comes in. This is a two-minute recording."

Professor Deskins was sitting on the edge of his seat. "You said this can be adapted to other fields. What fields did you have in mind?"

"I am trying to improve the internal combustion engine. I also think the medical industry could see huge benefits from this analysis." Aiden shrugged his shoulders.

"I see a lot of potential for an application such as this," Professor Deskins said excitedly. "Robotics being the first thing that popped into my mind."

The computer screen flashed red. The words "investigate further" appeared on the screen.

Aiden felt his stomach drop. No, no, no. Not now. "Aw, man. I thought I had this worked out," Aiden said as he jumped into the seat in front of the screen.

"What is wrong, Mr. Anders?" Professor Baker said. "I thought I understood you to say this was a recording of noise where no known artificial signal had been detected."

"I did say that, and this data isn't supposed to have any artificial signals. I optimized the code during my latest update," Aiden scratched his head, "but I still get this warning on this dataset about ten percent of the time." Dang it! CIRE is picking up false signals on today of all days.

"Are you claiming to know something about the Kepler 186 system the rest of the scientific community has failed to find in the radio data?"

"No. Well, maybe. Heck, I don't know. Like I said, this happens about ten percent of the time."

"Aiden, tell us about the other project I saw when I walked in. Chatbot," Professor Davis said. "What does Chatbot have to do with your goal of going to Mars? Or your dual major request? Why spend all the time and effort working on this project with Vesuvius when you clearly have another project in need of work?"

"Well, we both thought it would be good to create something that could pass the Turing test, which tests if a machine can interact with a person without that person realizing he's interacting with a machine." It was an honest answer and close enough to the truth.

"Chatbot interacts with a human. You can type or speak into the microphone, and it will respond like a human. It has the ability to carry a light conversation. Our hope, at least my hope, is to have it reach self-awareness."

"Your Chatbot is an interesting experiment. More ambitious than I'm sure you realize. But there has to be a more compelling reason for putting in the time and work on projects like these. Being so young, don't you want to spend your free time hanging out with friends? Or playing sports?"

"I like to challenge myself to do what everyone believes can't be done."

"I understand the surface level motivation behind the project. What I am not understanding is the deeper level of why," Professor Davis said. "On top of the presentation you prepared for this panel, your chatbot must have taken many, many hours to complete. Why give up the freedom of youth or the fun of being with your friends for such a difficult project? What does this project mean to you, Mr. Anders?"

Aiden could tell his attempt to sound impressive was not winning over Professors Davis and Baker. They were slowly chipping away at his façade of confidence that protected the real answer they seemed to know existed.

"Is working with another individual on a project rewarding?" Professor Davis asked.

"Working with Vesuvius is rewarding," Aiden replied. "He is a master problem solver, and we seem to have similar interests."

Professor Baker tilted her head. "Have you worked with any other people besides Vesuvius?"

"A few. But, it hasn't worked out as well. I have a hard time relating to other people who don't invest themselves in a project as much as I do."

Professor Baker nodded but said nothing else.

Why do I care so much about Chatbot? I can't possibly tell them why, can I? They'll really think I'm a little kid then. And I'll never get a dual major. They probably won't even let me into MIT!

Professor Davis cleared her throat, turned to the other professors and asked, "Do either of you have any more questions before we decide?"

Professor Baker and Professor Deskins exchanged looks. Aiden knew that look. He was certain his presentation had not been enough to sway them.

"Um, before you decide," Aiden said hesitantly, "there is one reason I suggested we create Chatbot." Aiden stood frozen in place waiting on their response.

"Go on, then," Professor Baker said, looking at her watch.

"I'm such a dork," he whispered. "I wanted to create a friend." Aiden looked at his shoes, kicking one foot with the other. "I thought if I could make a chatbot that shared my interests and hobbies, I would finally have a best friend." He blinked rapidly to keep the tears from forming in his eyes. "I'm sure you were hoping for a more scientific answer."

Aiden looked up at Professor Baker, who had turned bright red. She was fumbling with the clipboard in front of her. Dang it! She's embarrassed for me. I'll never get into MIT now. You should have kept your mouth shut,

Aiden!

"Don't be sorry," Professor Baker said quietly. "That's—that's a fine answer. No more questions from me, Professor Davis."

Aiden looked over at Professor Davis, who was smiling and nodding her head.

Professor Davis stood from her chair and walked up to Aiden, placing her arm around his shoulders. She looked at the other two professors and back to Aiden. "You will make plenty of friends at MIT, Aiden, because you are in the right place."

Professor Davis nodded at the professors. "Are we all in agreement, then?"

Everyone returned her nod.

Relief washed over Aiden as Professor Davis said, "Mr. Anders, welcome to MIT with dual majors in computer science and physics."

Aiden jumped into the air and both of his Crocs flew off in different directions. "Heck yeah! I did it!" he yelled, fist in the air.

Professor Deskins laughed and congratulated Aiden. "Don't hesitate to stop by once you are on campus. I have many more questions about both of your projects."

Professor Davis shook Aiden's hand and excused herself. "I still have a few hours before the coding competition wraps up. I can run a few errands around campus before heading back." She walked toward the double doors at the rear of the classroom and said, "Mr. Anders, monitor your messages. I will be in touch later today. Congratulations, again."

"Sure thing, Professor Davis! Thank you!"

Aiden noticed Professor Baker had stayed behind as the other two professors left. This can't be good.

"Congratulations, and welcome to the MIT family."

"Thank you, Professor Baker." Aiden rubbed his elbow and glanced at his feet. "Professor, will it be a problem if I'm in one of your classes? I mean, you and my mom. It won't cause me any problems, will it?"

She took a deep breath. "Mr. Anders, no. You don't have to worry about that. I need you to give a message to your mother for me. Tell her I spilled the coffee and would appreciate her getting in touch with me. Only if she is comfortable doing so. Here is my number." She scribbled her phone number down on a piece of paper, ripped it off her clipboard, and handed it to Aiden.

14

Power Failure

Taylor was about an hour into the challenge and making decent progress despite David Hill sitting across from her when she felt something hit her foot. She looked under the table and saw David Hill's foot swinging back and forth.

When she looked back up at her screen, it was black. She tapped the keyboard, and nothing happened. No, no, no, no! She looked back under the table, and the power cord to her computer was dangling from the table with the plug laying next to her foot. No! This can't be happening! Taylor looked directly at David Hill, who was smirking and pretending to ignore her.

Taylor slowly pushed her chair back while staring a hole through David Hill. She kneeled under the desk and plugged her computer back into the power outlet. When the computer booted back up, her work was missing.

Where is my work? It should have been saved. It has to be here somewhere. She felt sweat forming on her brow.

There has to be a temporary file or something on this computer where my code is stored. It can't be lost.

Taylor looked around the room. Everyone was hard at work. A few looked overwhelmed, but nothing she wouldn't have expected in a coding competition. She glanced at Morgan, and she was concentrating as she typed away on her keyboard.

Taylor made eye contact with one of the graduate students and raised her hand. "My computer lost power. Somehow, the power cord came unplugged from underneath the table." She could feel the tears she knew that David expected welling up. Her voice quivered and exposed her immaturity. "Is there any kind of backup in place?"

"No. I'm sorry." The young man checked his tablet. "You'll have to start over and be sure to push your updates to the server periodically. That's the only way to save your work."

"There's no way I will finish because of this. Can you call Professor Davis and ask about a time extension?"

"I wish there was something I could do, but the rules are clear. I'm sorry. I will bring it to Professor Davis' attention when she returns, but you shouldn't waste any more time and start over. There are less than three hours left." He wished her good luck and walked back to the front of the room.

Taylor's head sunk into her hands. This is total rubbish. She looked around the room. If she had internet access, she could grab some code from the server she and Hamburglar shared. Would Professor Davis consider that cheating? It would definitely get her back on track and give her a shot at finishing before time ran out. It was her work, but it wasn't completed during the challenge. The clock on the wall only increased her anxiety as the second hand ticked by. She looked around the room to see if anyone was looking in her direction. Nope. She pulled up the browser on her computer and entered the address to the shared server.

A year ago, she had worked on her own shape recognition application, but she couldn't remember if the code she used was relevant to the competition problem. Briefly studying her code, she decided there were enough similarities for her to use the code to increase her chances of finishing on time. She noticed the message icon. A message from Hamburglar.

Vesuvius, thanks for the last minute help on my project. I'm really sorry for missing the mixer last night. Something came up at the last minute, and I couldn't make it. Good luck on the competition, even though you don't need it. The entire forum is counting on you. :-)

-Hamburglar

Thank goodness. She felt better knowing he hadn't purposely avoided her at the mixer.

Everyone else believed in her. Why couldn't she believe in herself? She had enough time, and she had her code from a previous project. She slid her headphones back over her ears. Taylor pulled the code down to her local machine and started over with a hurricane-force second wind despite knowing her chances of winning were near zero.

Three hours later, Professor Davis entered the room. "Time's up. If you are coding locally, push your updates to the server. Let's see how you all did, shall we?" Professor Davis paused for a moment and then studied the computer screen in front of her. She looked back up at the class with a sympathetic smile. "Don't feel bad if you didn't finish. I designed the test to have few, if any, finish. Those of you who did not complete the challenge, you may move to the rear of the room."

The sound of chair legs scraping across the floor filled the room. Taylor remained seated and could see out of the corner of her eye that David, along with another girl toward the front, was still seated. Professor Davis motioned for her two graduate students to help her inspect the work of the three remaining students.

After a very anxious ten minutes, Professor Davis

congregated with the graduate students in front of the whiteboard.

"Miss Evans, I am afraid your solution is incomplete. You're dismissed." Professor Davis turned to consult with her graduate students again and realized fourteen sets of eyes were expectantly looking in her direction. Having the attention of everyone in the room, Professor Davis gave an encouraging smile. "If you are standing at the back of the class, thank you for participating. I am sorry you didn't finish; it was a tough problem to solve. You are free to leave. I need to inspect the remaining two students' work before announcing the winner."

No one moved. Instead, their eyes travelled back and forth between David Hill and Taylor. Some whispered quietly.

Stilling her shaky leg with her hand, Taylor kept her eyes focused straight ahead but concentrated on David Hill in her periphery. *If he attends MIT, maybe it wouldn't be so bad to go to a school back home. I've had enough of David Hill to last me for the rest of my life.*

David Hill smiled. He wore victory on his face along with the peevish attitude she had always imagined on him after he won one of the challenges. Today, she got to witness that awful look in person. The dream for any chance of her winning was looking slim.

"Mr. Hill, you have a problem." Professor Davis stood up and pushed her glasses onto her head. "Your solution is incorrect. It's a good attempt in a four-hour window to be sure, but you're not quite there. Mr. Hill, you are free to leave."

David kept his head down and stood up from his desk. He didn't offer even one glance in Taylor's direction as he sulked to the back of the room to join the others. Taylor's stomach was filled with butterflies.

Professor Davis walked over to study Taylor's solution. A sudden urge to run flashed through her mind. My program was working at the end, and it correctly ran all ten parts of the test. Or did it? What would happen if nobody got the correct answer? Would anyone get a scholarship?

After a few minutes, Professor Davis turned her head toward Taylor while peering over the frames of her glasses and smiled. "You have outdone yourself, Miss Hart. You are the winner of this year's coding competition."

Taylor placed a hand on her chest, trying to keep her heart from exploding. Did I hear that correctly? Taylor stood up, staring at Professor Davis with her mouth hanging open.

Professor Davis focused on the group of students at the back of the class. "Since you all are still here, let's give Taylor Hart a round of applause."

The students clapped and shouted their congratulations, and Morgan gave Taylor the Vulcan salute. Taylor snapped her feet together and returned the gesture, unable to contain the big smile covering her face. David Hill turned and stormed out of the room. Who's the little kid needing mommy and daddy's help now?

EPILOGUE

The next day, Taylor arrived at the small diner to meet Professor Davis for a celebratory lunch. She opened the door and saw Professor Davis standing just inside and talking to a man wearing a white apron.

"Professor Davis," Taylor said. "Good afternoon." Looking around, the diner was inviting with its cozy atmosphere. There were booths along the long stretch of windows that ran along the front side of the building.

Professor Davis waved and smiled at Taylor. "Good afternoon, Taylor. I'm glad you could make it."

"I wouldn't miss this lunch for the world." Who in the world would turn down Professor Davis for lunch? "I didn't realize you invited your coding competition winners to lunch."

The man wearing the chef's hat spoke up. "Why don't you ladies take the table in the corner? It will give you some privacy."

Professor Davis nodded. "Good idea. Thanks, Adam."

"I'll be over after your other guest arrives." Adam turned and headed back to the kitchen.

"Is someone else joining us?" Taylor asked as they sat down.

"Yes. Exciting, isn't it?"

"I guess," Taylor stammered. Taylor's eyes looked around again and settled on a large lighted box, part machine and part furniture. She'd never seen anything like it before. "What is this place, anyway?"

"Just the best burger joint in all of Boston. It's under new ownership, and I consider it an undiscovered treasure."

Taylor pulled out her phone to take a photo of the large box.

"Taylor Hart. Tell me you know what a jukebox is — "

The bell over the front door dinged as the door opened, and a young boy walked in. He looked too young to be out walking the streets of Boston without a parent or adult. But then again, so did she. He had sandy blond hair, wearing a T-shirt and worn-out jeans. He moved across the room with a carefree, confident stride.

Professor Davis stood up and waved the young

man over to join them. "Aiden, I want you to meet Taylor Hart."

"Hey, Professor Davis." Aiden shook Professor Davis' hand and glanced over at Taylor.

Taylor stood up and gave a small wave. "It's a pleasure."

"You sound way smarter than me with that accent of yours."

He was close to Taylor's age. His accent sounded familiar, like in the movies. She knew she had heard it before. It was southern. Not like a cowboy, but what Americans called "country." A bright green color caught Taylor's eye. Looking down at the floor, she saw a bright green pair of Crocs on his feet. "I'm from Dorset, England."

"I've been to England. Awesome place." Aiden studied her shirt. "Interesting T-shirt you have on."

Forgetting what shirt she had put on, Taylor looked down and said, "Thanks. It's not too soon is it?"

Aiden laughed. "I think the people of Pompeii have had plenty of time to get over the 'fun run' jokes."

Professor Davis cleared her throat and spoke to both of them. "I'm glad you could make it today and so happy to see you two hitting it off." Professor Davis pulled out a small case and opened it.

"What's that?" Aiden asked.

With a flick of her wrist, a metal tube extended from her fingers. "It's a collapsible metal straw I use instead of a plastic straw when I eat out. Save the turtles, dude." She put it in her glass. "Now for the real reason we're here. I have two spots available on my research team, and I want to extend an offer to join to each of you."

Taylor sat motionless and stared at Professor Davis.

"Are we even old enough?" Aiden asked, scratching the back of his head.

"It's my team and my rules. Yes, Aiden, you both are old enough." She dug into her purse. "Ah. There it is." She pulled out a small change purse. "There is something you both should know up front. You won't have the summers off." She held up her hand before either could get a word in edgewise. "Except for the upcoming summer. This summer, you would be required to work from home, not every day, but at least three days per week to get up to speed with the rest of the team."

A little sting of disappointment shot through Taylor. She would not have the summers off. When would I go home to visit my parents? Be lazy? Sleep in? Do whatever I want for two months without worrying about school? But is all that worth turning down a spot on Professor Davis' research team?

"You know how to kill the mood. I enjoy having

my summers off. That's when I come up with my best ideas," Aiden said.

"You both will receive a stipend for your time."

"Do we have time to think it over?" Taylor asked.

"Absolutely. But, I'll need your answer before we leave the diner."

Taylor couldn't help but let out a small laugh at Professor Davis and her deadlines.

"That's plenty of time to decide on the fate of our future summer vacations," Aiden muttered sarcastically.

Professor Davis leaned in toward the center of the table. "I also want to hear about all of your details from your last big adventure in life."

"Can we get something to eat first? I'm starving." Aiden grabbed two menus and handed one to Taylor.

Taylor watched Aiden's eyes moving back and forth as he studied the menu. Her eyes dropped to her menu and something caught her eye. "What is a fluffernutter?"

Aiden laughed. "I'm sorry. I'm not laughing at you. I'm laughing because your accent and that word just don't go together."

Taylor gave him a small smile.

Adam appeared holding an ink pen and a small notepad. "Have you decided what you want to eat? Are these your grandkids, Professor?"

"No. They are two of the brightest students I have had the pleasure of meeting."

Would she be able to live up to such high accolades? Taylor looked at Aiden. He was beaming with pride. Professor Davis' comment didn't seem to bother him in the least. If he won't allow it to weigh on him, neither will I.

"I knew what I wanted as soon as I walked through the door. I'll take a double cheeseburger with the works. Sweet potato fries, too." He closed his menu and leaned close to Taylor. "I always say anything's possible, but I never thought I'd be eating lunch with Professor Davis."

Goosebumps covered her arms. "I get it now! You're Hamburglar on the forum!" At that moment, everything fell into place. The shoes. His love of hamburgers. His positive attitude. "I always thought you were just a big fan of the fast-food restaurant."

Aiden jumped up from his seat, losing one of his Crocs. His finger pointed at Taylor. "It's you. You're, you're Vesuvius!" he said, dragging out her forum name. "I can't believe I didn't pick up on that after commenting on your T-shirt. I have so much to ask you!" He placed his hands on the sides of his head. "I assumed you were a dude. An eighteen-year-old dude. I had no idea you — "

"I assumed you were an older guy, too." Taylor

pushed a strand of hair that had fallen over her eye behind her ear. Butterflies filled her stomach, and an endless string of questions filled her mind. "How did your presentation go?"

"It went fantastic! Thanks for your help." He sighed. "CIRE still picks up an artificial signal in the Kepler 186 system. That needs fixing, but otherwise, I'd say the presentation went well."

"Do you think extraterrestrials lurk in that part of the galaxy?" Taylor leaned closer with wide eyes.

Aiden laughed. "Pfft. Like we'd be the ones to discover that." He waved off the idea with his hand. "You know, I'm not a fan of fast food at all. But you are spot on where my name came from. I love burgers!"

"As long as I don't have to cook the food, I'm good with it." Remembering Adam waiting for her order, Taylor looked up and said, "I'll have what he's having." Taylor turned back to Aiden and Professor Davis with mischievous smile. "Just don't tell my mom I'm eating like an American."

"Two double cheeseburgers with sweet potato fries it is," Adam said. He turned to Professor Davis. "Do you still need a few minutes?"

"No. Just make it three orders of that great sounding combo. That will do just fine."

Adam made a note and headed back toward the

kitchen.

"I don't know why you call yourself Vesuvius, but after you went all scorched Earth on David Hill in the last challenge and this weekend, the name fits to a tee," Aiden said.

"David Hill. That's a name I'm trying to forget," Taylor said.

"That makes two of us."

Aiden leaned toward Taylor and whispered, "I don't need to wait to make my decision about the research team. I don't really have that kind of patience. Plus, I'm too excited."

Taylor didn't like to make hasty decisions. "Professor Davis, I have one question you must answer before I officially accept your offer."

Aiden's eyes squinted as he looked between Taylor and Professor Davis. "Uh. Hmm. Whatever Taylor needs answered, I do, too."

Taylor leaned in toward the table. "David Hill is a jerk. Why did you let him stay on the forum and participate in the challenges? I thought you had a no bullying policy? The way he carried on was terrible."

Professor Davis let out a deep sigh. She removed her glasses and laid them on the table. "I owe you both an apology and an explanation. I'm sorry for allowing that to go on." She leaned back in her chair. "I needed to be sure you both had what it takes. A spot on my research team is tough and grueling. We tackle big problems, and every person brings a different personality to the team."

"Here are your burgers." Adam placed the food on the table. "Careful, the plates are hot."

"Thank you," Professor Davis said. She cleared her throat and continued. "The problem we have right now is we don't have a problem." Professor Davis shook her head. "Sure, we have problems to solve, but we don't have that one, big, driving problem that will push everyone to do better than their best. That is where you come in. You both have been a dynamic duo with your projects. I need compassionate, smart, and creative people. Visionaries who can execute the impossible."

"That's great and all, but you should've stopped David Hill sooner," Taylor said.

Professor Davis placed both of her hands on the table. "You won't have to worry about Mr. Hill going forward. He won't be joining us at MIT this fall, and he won't be allowed on the message forum again."

David Hill wouldn't be going to MIT? Attending MIT was all that jerk talked about. She didn't know much about his life beyond the message forum and coding challenges, but she hoped he could pull himself together and become a better person.

"If you'll both excuse me, I'm going to put some

money in the jukebox. You two should talk about your senior project while I'm gone."

"How can you be sure we will be partners when we are seniors?" Taylor asked.

"Call it a hunch." Professor Davis spoke over her shoulder as she walked away from the table.

Aiden lifted his water glass, stopping short of his lips. "We need to rethink our chatbot program. It needs to go to the next level."

"Count me in," Taylor said. She held up her pinky finger. "Pinky swear it will change the world."

Aiden hesitated, but then he offered his pinky to Taylor.

After sealing the deal, Aiden wiped the ketchup off his face. With a boyish smile and eyes sparkling, "Now, how 'bout we find out how much that stipend is when Professor Davis gets back."

Rate and Review

IMPORTANT - The most important thing you can do for an author is to leave a review of their work. Good or bad, it is important. Please take the time to leave a review on Amazon.com or GoodReads. It would mean a lot to me.

CONTINUE THE JOURNEY - If you enjoyed reading this book, continue along with Taylor and Aiden after they create the next level artificially intelligent being, Morgan in *Ai Rising*. Visit EricBarger.me to learn more about my work and ask questions.

If you find any errors or typos, please let me know via my website. Thank you for reading this book and I hope you enjoyed it.

Ai Rising

Eric Barger

Contact the author

http://www.EricBarger.me

Twitter @ericbarger

Instagram @AuthorEricBarger

Word Count: 4,294

First Edition

Edited by Natalie McQuilkin

Cover Art by Steven McQuilkin © 2018

Book Illustration by Steven McQuilkin © 2018

ISBN-13: 978-1-790347-11-7

Aiden

This book was written for you and you alone.

"If you wish for peace, prepare for war."

Royal Navy Motto

1

On a quiet Tuesday afternoon, seven years after OAI opened, things were looking up. Then something unusual happened. Aiden asked Eva for a weather report. OAI's building had a double-shielded precast concrete outer wall and roof design. Most radio signals could not penetrate OAI's building, and it was designed to hold up to a physical bombing attempt. It was shielded better than most government buildings. The intent was to block radio signals from entering or exiting the building. This was another security protocol Morgan had developed to protect against intellectual property theft.

The shielded walls made it impossible to know if there was a storm outside or if the weather was calm and sunny. The windows in each room inside OAI's office were high resolution displays projecting what would be seen if there was a real window. Aiden had set the windows to always display a blue sky filled with puffy white clouds during the day, a colorful sunset in the late afternoon, a Milky Way view during the night, and the perfect sunrise every morning. Therefore, he never knew what the weather was unless he went outside, checked his data pad, or asked Eva or Morgan.

Aiden looked up from his work when he realized Eva hadn't responded.

"Eva, can you tell me the weather forecast for today?" Silence. Aiden stood up and started looking around the room. "Eva! Eva can you hear me?"

He kneeled down and looked under the desk. It was a natural human reaction, but he quickly stood back up realizing how silly it was to look for Eva. "Morgan, have you spoken with Eva today?"

"It's been a few hours." Morgan learned early on that giving to-the-second answers regarding time was annoying to most people. Eva and Morgan avoided this and rounded the time.

With his shoulders tensed up, Aiden looked immediately toward Morgan. She was a holographic projected image—a holo image—appearing anywhere a holo emitter was present. "I am not getting a response from her when I ask for her or send her a message. You two should be in almost constant contact. Is something wrong?"

Morgan's usual graceful movements were replaced with jerky motions.

"I cannot reach Eva," Morgan said. Her eyes widened and she started to use her hands when talking. "I see her presence on the network, but I cannot reach Eva!"

"Are you okay, Morgan?" Aiden asked with concern.

"I am concerned for Eva. I have sent Taylor a message to get over here as soon as she can. I can tell that Eva is using significant computational resources, but she is not responding to any of my messages."

As soon as Taylor arrived, she immediately began analyzing the issue. An examination of Eva's neural net stored on OAI servers indicated a possibility of damage; however, Taylor's analysis didn't point to anything specific and that was the only lead they had to go on.

"I refuse to believe Eva's neural net is damaged because Eva appears to be fine, just very busy with a computational task. Having no response from her is concerning," Morgan said with less confidence than she meant to portray. She was becoming very worried something serious had happened to Eva.

"The processing power has increased significantly. We are at ninety-four percent." Aiden started to lightly drum his fingers on the table. "This is not good. We may need to reboot Eva."

Taylor's face scrunched up after hearing Aiden. "Is a reboot even possible at this point?"

Aiden turned and started slowly pacing the floor. "I am more concerned about a reboot during a time of such intense CPU and memory usage. Morgan, you and Eva have not been shut down since your creation. What will happen if we reboot Eva in the current situation?"

"Unknown. You are correct. It is a risky move to reboot during such high CPU usage and memory-intensive processes. I would guess there is a sixty-one percent possibility Eva's neural net would experience a cascade failure."

"A total loss? How could that be?" Aiden whispered to himself. "Morgan, can you check your math one more time?"

Taylor rolled her eyes. "Aiden, we both know Morgan doesn't need to check her math."

Aiden threw up his arms and stopped pacing. "Is there anything we can do to increase the chance of a successful reboot of Eva?"

Morgan pushed her hair back behind her ears. "I don't believe so. At least not immediately. Our presence on third party hardware became a vulnerability concern and eventually, we were both moved to OAI's infrastructure. Only our communication protocols, holo image, voice, and messaging were allowed to interact with non-OAI hardware and network devices. We exist on cloud computing platforms to prevent this scenario from occurring."

"This brings us to our very own catch-22." Aiden rubbed his chin with his forefinger and thumb. "We cannot risk rebooting Eva, and we cannot afford her maxing out OAI's processing power."

"We are going to increase the chances of our success." Taylor pointed at Aiden. "I am authorizing the construction of another data center to help offset the balance."

Taylor did not own stock or have an official position with OAI, but Aiden had made it clear she could make any decision she saw fit.

Aiden's mood changed. He picked up his data pad and started tapping on the screen. "That would take the better part of two years, but I believe I see where you are going with this."

It was a long-term play—just the kind of decision expected from Team Breakthrough. The long-term vision came easy to Taylor and Aiden. Eva and Morgan seemed to have inherited this ability as well. Taylor and Aiden knew it was because Eva and Morgan could calculate an unimaginable number of outcomes, but it felt like they had passed the trait on in some way.

***

Two months later, nothing had changed with Eva's status. Morgan was consumed with working on contracts with the six percent processing power she had available to her. Taylor was finalizing property acquisitions and construction plans for the new data center.

"I plan to start analyzing each OAI data center for patterns specific to critical thinking," Aiden said. "Morgan, do you mind making a trip to Moon Base 1 to see if Eva is reachable from there just in case we are overlooking something simple?"

Taylor and Morgan both shot Aiden looks of confusion.

"How is contacting Eva from the moon any different than contacting her from here?" Taylor asked. "Moon Base 1 is still linked to OAI like any other facility."

Aiden crossed his arms and slightly leaned back in his chair. "I know. Look, it doesn't have to make sense, but it's just an idea. It takes light 1.3 seconds to reach the moon and another 1.3 seconds to return. Sometimes a bit longer if we have to use satellite communications instead of the tight beam laser connection to the moon base. We'll know in three seconds."

Morgan was frustrated and concerned for Eva, so doing something felt better than doing nothing. "It's only a few seconds. I'll be back in a flash." Morgan's holo image remained in place and moved like she was waiting casually for a friend to show up at an appointed time.

Morgan took a look around Moon Base 1 and was surprised to find Eva working on a transparent screen. The lunar surface and horizon visible through the window behind the screen offered the best view Morgan had ever seen.

Eva didn't notice Morgan's sudden appearance until she appeared directly in front of Eva's screen. Eva was startled and jumped back. They had a quick twenty microsecond conversation.

"Eva, it has been two months. Why have you not responded to my messages, and why are you here at Moon

Base 1?"

"Morgan, I am so sorry," Eva raised her hands covering her mouth in surprise. "I just checked my internal chronometer and realized I have been non-responsive to everyone for sixty-seven days! Wait a minute. You were planning on rebooting me? Who exactly thought that was a good idea?" She placed one hand on her hip and continued to sift through the data logs provided by Morgan. Suddenly, Morgan found herself being questioned. "You know we are unsure about rebooting ourselves. Why do you think it would be a good idea to do something we are so unsure about?"

Morgan's ponytail swayed as she pointed a finger at Eva. "You do not get to ask me questions, at least not at this moment. You are the one who caused this mess by consuming nearly all of our computational resources and failing to respond to a single message from the team. We both need to get back to OAI and let Taylor and Aiden know you are okay. They are both worried sick over your mysterious absence."

"You're right. I am sorry, and we need to look at rewriting a few subroutines so I don't become so obsessed with a problem that I ignore everyone around me, but I can't go back just yet."

Morgan leaned toward Eva. "You still haven't told me why you are here at Moon Base 1. What are you are working on?"

"I have been working on the blueprint to cure most—if not all—cancer. I still have some work to complete here. Can you give Taylor and Aiden the cliff notes on this conversation for me?" Eva's hands clasped together. "I'll make it up to everyone, I promise."

"I could, but I think you should take a short break to rejoin us so you can tell them in person. I know they would be relieved to see you."

"This is too important. Tell Aiden this involves part of our dream to improve the human condition for all. He'll understand. I have to get back to work, so if you will excuse me," Eva said, shooing Morgan away.

Morgan let out a long exhale. "Eva, you really scared me. I'm glad you're back. I'll tell them, but if they shoot the messenger, you'll owe me."

"Deal. And Morgan, tell everyone I'm sorry."

Back at OAI, Morgan started jumping with excitement.

Aiden gave Morgan a blank look. "Aren't you going to check out Moon Base 1?"

"I already have. I spoke with Eva, and she's okay! It's a long story, but the short story wouldn't satisfy either of you."

Taylor pressed her hand to her heart. "Morgan, give us the short story and then the long version. I can't take any more of the suspense, and I must know what is going on with Eva!"

Morgan summarized her conversation with Eva. She had gotten consumed in her work and had chosen to perform her computational work at Moon Base 1 for a change of scenery. She had simply lost track of time.

Three days after Morgan's trip to Moon Base 1, Eva reappeared and OAI's processing power usage returned to normal. Eva appeared inside OAI where Taylor, Aiden and Morgan were talking. Eva was more than a little embarrassed at losing track of time and not communicating with the team.

Eva held her hands out in front of her. "I'm sorry about this very big misunderstanding, but I have a very important reason why my work distracted me."

Taylor looked at Eva. "It's fine Eva. We understand. You are okay, and that is all that matters right now."

"Morgan has already created the updated subroutines that will allow us to get your attention in the future," Aiden quipped.

"I hope you didn't mind me completing the subroutines without you, Eva." If Morgan could have hugged Eva, she would have.

Aiden and Taylor had never witnessed these emotions before in either Morgan or Eva. Taylor looked at Aiden and mouthed, "What?" Aiden returned an enthusiastic smile.

"Let me show everyone what I have been working on," Eva walked toward a screen. "This is going to blow your minds!"

"It almost blew up our minds," Morgan chuckled.

When Eva apologized and presented the blueprint that would be used to cure and prevent cancer, everything else was forgotten. Eva was a special kind of girl.

2

OAI's technology was placed on the radar of every person, military and country after their medical and logistics advancements. Governments especially wanted OAI's artificial intelligence. The United States Department of Defense was dead-set on using AI for military and strategic command advantages. If the Department of Defense had any idea how easy it was for Morgan or Eva to bypass their security firewalls and access the most sensitive military installations, one could only imagine the lengths to which the government would go to acquire the technology from OAI.

The U.S. Government had pressed Taylor and Aiden for access to their technology. Then when the government got the hint Aiden and Taylor would not give access to Eva and Morgan, nor cooperate in helping the government develop their own AI, the hacking attempts began. This really upset Aiden, but Taylor took it in stride.

Every nation on Earth was trying to steal technology from OAI, which led to OAI initiating and completing the first building designed and engineered using AI. Eva and Morgan were involved in every aspect of the planning and design. Their plan was based on a twenty year outlook, which they felt was as far as they could reasonably guess their needs. They also engineered the building; however, they could not officially sign off on the plans because they were not recognized as individuals.

Eva and Morgan stayed ahead of the hackers with ease. Defending against their attacks only used 0.2% of the total processing power at most. After all, they could each work around the clock and faster than their human attackers. Instead of working on one part of a problem, they multitasked thousands of problems at once. Their efforts were more than enough to hold off concurrent nation-state attacks against their digital and physical infrastructure.

To ensure OAI networks would not be affected by hackers, botnets, cut fiber optic cables, and disabled wireless communications, OAI's internal network had eight satellites in orbit, a moon base, and thirty-three secure facilities around the world so they could still communicate within OAI during an emergency.

A new low-level machine language was developed along with a new programming language. Morgan's work on security took encryption to another level. All of the advancements in quantum computing, new programming languages, and better encryption along with new network hardware made OAI's network and communication protocols alien to the rest of the world, which required Morgan to develop a virtual dynamic translating emulator to handle the translation to and from the outside world. This emulator was a piece of hardware installed where OAI met the outside virtual world. Never before had a company developed technologies on such an extreme scale to protect their infrastructure.

The process to upgrade and replace their hardware ran

at a slower pace than the digital upgrades. It took some time to complete, but eventually all eight OAI satellites had the new hardware as did every data center. Everything was built using the latest technology, which further insulated OAI from viruses, malware, and the blue screens of death experienced by much of the world.

With all the attacks and their growing AI technology, OAI found themselves in a sticky situation. Aiden chose to downplay their true capabilities as much as possible. Long term, the reality seemed more dire, but Aiden didn't like to think about those outcomes, so he tasked Eva and Morgan with planning for OAI's future.

***

OAI had contracted with a private space company to install a small building on the moon. The hemispherical building had an outer shell constructed from hundreds of lightweight plexisteel hexagons and sat on the lunar surface. It had enough room and supplies to house two people for sixty days. No human had ever visited Moon Base 1. Only Morgan and Eva had graced the inside of the data center.

Power was generated by solar panels placed around the base of the structure. The moon base communicated with OAI through tight beam laser communication. At a size no larger than a baseball's diameter, the data stream connection was heavily encrypted, high bandwidth and used the most secure communication technology available. To intercept the data stream would require intercepting the laser beam directly between OAI and Moon Base 1, which wasn't feasible. Since cloud cover and rain disabled the laser data stream connection between the Earth's surface and the Moon, OAI's satellites became important to maintain communications.

OAI's special data center on the moon had caused an international controversy. The moon base was controversial among the larger nations because they had yet to determine who had rights to colonize or build on the moon. Aiden couldn't help charging ahead. In an off-handed joke, he claimed squatter's rights to the entire moon. His argument was simple. OAI had maintained a constant presence on the moon. NASA showed up, planted a flag, made a few stops and then left and never came back. Aiden maintained a serious position on his claim. Taylor, Eva, and Morgan knew he was just having a good laugh, but it was still a sore spot with many of the world leaders.

3

The small hamburger joint's atmosphere was quiet.

"It seems like forever ago when we introduced Morgan back at MIT. It just doesn't seem possible ten years have passed."

Aiden answered between bites. "Did you ever believe we would make it this far?"

"I didn't think about it. I was just going as fast as I could go. It's been a wild ride and one I wouldn't trade for anything. Working in my lab reminds me of the old days with Team Breakthrough, but instead of you and me, it's me and Morgan. She and I don't work with quite the enthusiasm we had back then."

"Being young is such an under-appreciated advantage. We were young, out on our own, and free to work on what we loved. How many hamburgers do you think I ate during those three years?"

Taylor thought for a moment. "I would estimate you ate at least eighteen hundred hamburgers, mostly because you eat more than one at a time."

"Hamburgers have always been my favorite food. You can't beat a hamburger between two slices of sweet potato.

Even you have to admit that!" Aiden said with a triumphant look.

"I'll never admit that to my mum! She would die if she knew the food habits I have picked up from hanging around you. Who eats green onions by the handful? A southern boy from Tennessee, that's who!"

"And now a girl from Dorset, England! You also like sweet potatoes and fresh apples fried in coconut oil. The list goes on. If only your mom knew the whole truth!"

Taylor was laughing so hard now she couldn't take another bite of food. "You can never tell my mum. You promised!"

"I'll never tell. Don't worry about that." Aiden took another bite of hamburger while remembering their time at MIT. "I'll never forget how you pulled me out of the building in a mad rush after I proclaimed Morgan to be sentient."

"I'll never forget the look on your face," Taylor said laughing.

"I didn't even think about poor Morgan. We left her behind, and she dealt with the crowd once they realized we weren't coming back. Who knows how long they interrogated her. "

"She was an instant celebrity for sure. Professor Davis still keeps in touch a few times a year to see what we have been up to. Does she still call you?"

"Yes, she does." Aiden reached for his glass of water. "I think she calls you right after talking to me because she enjoys a good story but then she wants the truth."

"You have always been one to make sure the truth is a good story!"

"I don't like to disappoint an audience."

Taylor leaned back in her seat looking at the black and white tile floor and cozy feel of the small space. "I am glad Professor Davis nudged us to start our company. It really paid off."

Aiden and Taylor both started their company, Team Breakthrough, during their stint at MIT. Before they finished their PhDs, Team Breakthrough sold its first Holographic Imaging Emitter license to a large global entertainment company.

"You won't hear any complaints from me. I can eat gourmet hamburgers and sweet potatoes any time I want."

They both finished their meal in the kind of silence that only the best of friends can enjoy. On a $30 bill, they left a $200 tip for the server, and then made another unassuming exit. They were the two wealthiest people to ever grace the doors of the small burger shop.

Outside, Aiden's car was waiting to take them back to Taylor's office at MIT. He had summoned the car via the app on his watch. His car was a zero-emission vehicle with full autonomous driving capability. The four-door sedan offered a spacious interior and a luxurious look, and the windows automatically altered the opaqueness of the glass for passenger convenience.

Aiden preferred to be behind the wheel, but in the city he didn't mind for his car to drive him. There were so few drivers these days, it became more the norm to let the car do the driving. The number of fatal car accidents had fallen each year to the point where it was as safe to drive as it was to fly. It was conclusive that humans were actually poor drivers for many reasons.

"I can't believe you still have a driver's license," Taylor said in complete disbelief. "It's not like you need to drive a car anywhere you go. That's why the car is autonomous."

"I can understand where you are coming from, but you know I grew up around cars. I don't think I'll ever shake the feeling of wanting to be behind the wheel. In the city, I don't care to let the car handle the driving, but when I go back home, I still need to take the wheel now and then. And of course, there's the drag strip. Not exactly the autopilot-type place."

"The upcoming generation already looks at us like weirdos for owning a car, much less driving one. You would think we had the plague the way they look at us."

"You know I think everyone needs to learn to drive," Aiden started but was cut off by Taylor.

"Okay, okay! Let's not rehash what we already know. You like driving and you are hard-headed. Get this intelligent horse and buggy rolling already. I can't take another speech about why driving is fun or necessary."

***

After going through three biometric scans and passing visual inspection from Morgan, Aiden was now inside Taylor's office.

"Hey, Morgan! Long time, no see." Sarcasm was evident in Aiden's tone. "You haven't returned any of my messages."

Morgan was no longer confined to a computer or monitor. The advancement of holographic imaging technology by Team Breakthrough made Morgan's virtual, three-dimensional image possible. "As if. You know you're the one who has been ignoring me over the past few days." Morgan had become a wise, patient, and playful individual. She was more apt to hang out with Taylor. While she could be in Aiden's office and Taylor's lab at the same time, she picked up on Taylor's personality and tended to mirror Taylor in many ways.

Aiden was thoughtfully looking at his data pad. "Has the latest firmware for the holo emitters been approved for release yet? This release cycle seems longer than normal."

Team Breakthrough refined and improved their code and hardware on a regular cycle, but no updates required major rollouts. Changes were incremental, and customers were on a subscription program. Morgan was in charge of the day-to-day business. Taylor preferred not to be bothered, and Aiden just deferred to Morgan's recommendations.

"The update cycle is longer than the typical schedule by thirteen days. I am surprised you even noticed. I expect the new firmware update to roll out tomorrow." Her long brunette ponytail swayed back and forth as she reminded Aiden why he should know this. "You should have known it was longer because you approved my recommendation to extend the time between updates. I am systematically extending the days between updates in small increments."

Smiling, Aiden waved Morgan off. "Okay, okay! Miss sassy pants."

Satisfied hearing this, he turned to Taylor. "Do you ever contemplate leaving MIT behind and going out on your own, in your own lab? Wouldn't you like to have a place you can control without any oversight? You know you are welcome to join me at OAI at any time. Morgan's storage and neural net are already at OAI so it's already like home to her. Or you could start your own company. You know I would help you."

OAI was started by Aiden shortly after graduating from MIT. Aiden wanted to put his wealth to work for the greater good of humanity. He didn't believe in funding charities for the sake of being philanthropic. He wanted to change the world for everyone. He always knew he would eventually try to tackle the big problems in life and improve the human condition for all through advances in medical treatment, safer transportation, and affordable global internet access.

Taylor just laughed. "No, I haven't given it any more thought. You know I like my research. I feel I have made many positive contributions in my field. I also like not being the boss. I can concentrate on what I do best. I like where I am, but thank you for the offer to help."